NIGHT SWORN

NIGHT SWORN

DRAGON OF SHADOW AND AIR BOOK FIVE

JESS MOUNTIFIELD

DISRUPTIVE IMAGINATION

LMBPN Publishing
PMB 196, 2540 South Maryland Pkwy
Las Vegas, NV 89109

Version 1.02 December 2021
eBook ISBN: 978-1-64971-903-4
Print ISBN: 978-1-64971-904-1

Dedication:

To any woman who was ever confident about something they were good at. And had it mistaken for arrogance.

CHAPTER ONE

The sunset over LA was always a sight that warmed my insides and made me feel alive. Sitting next to Zephyr and watching it was the highlight of my evenings. It also helped that the builders who were extending the warehouse space had left half an hour before the light show began.

For now, the roof was quiet again. With any luck, it would be permanently soon. Around Zephyr and me were the half-finished walls and rooms that would become the bedrooms of most of the residents here.

At the moment, Zephyr and I were sitting off to one side, where the sloped roof entrance had been constructed already, designed for us to land on the roof, slip through a hatch large enough for my growing dragon and then walk farther into the building.

"It never grows old, does it?" Minsheng's voice came from behind. I looked back to notice Zephyr had already turned. I'd been too distracted to pick up on Zephyr's attention shifting elsewhere.

I think we're both distracted, Zephyr said. *He got up onto the roof before I noticed him.*

"It's the first moment of peace we've had all day," I replied, turning back to the view and moving over so my Shishou could come and sit beside us.

"Yes, Chris and Daisy asked me to congratulate you on the stroke of genius it was ordering takeaway for the protesters outside, Aella," Minsheng said as he lowered himself to the floor and the cushion I'd found.

"It worked, then?"

"Quietest they've been all week."

"Do they know we bought it for them?" I asked, grinning.

"I figured I'd let them work it out on their own. If they're going to be angry that we bought them something when they don't like us, they might as well be fed first, and if it's going to do anything to change their opinion of us, not blowing our own trumpet will only make it have an even bigger impact on them." Minsheng gazed out at the sky as he spoke, prompting me to do the same.

The sun was pretty much down over the bay, and the sky was growing darker overhead. It wouldn't be long before we could sneak off to the beach without anyone following us and practice some of our flying techniques.

"When you get back, we're going to have to discuss what we're going to do. We can't really work while having all these protesters outside the warehouse," Minsheng said a few minutes later.

"I know," I replied. "Lyra has mentioned that it's beginning to eat into the dojo's income, and I don't want her business to suffer because of me."

I shook my head as I thought back to the event that had started all our problems. When a group of soldiers and agents commanded by Jacobs had gone to try and track down the Sanctuary and kill every mythical in the protected area, I'd led some of those very mythicals into battle and ambushed the attackers on the way.

Only two years ago I'd been a regular Jane, and I'd honestly believed I was doing the right thing when I'd started the attack. However, the media and Jacobs had spun the footage they had of it, and I'd been painted to be a violent murderer. Very few soldiers had been badly hurt or killed compared to several dead mythicals, but it hadn't mattered to a number of US citizens.

As I thought about it, a weight settled inside me. I'd been one of them once. I'd been just another American getting on with life and trying to live the American dream. And merely because I'd dared to stand up for those who needed protection and to be treated fairly, I'd been turned into a public enemy.

"There's got to be some way to show them I mean no harm to anyone as long as we're left in peace," I said a moment later, feeling tears sting my eyes.

Pushing the emotion away, I got up and walked to the far edge of the roof. As soon as I could see the protesters, I stopped and tucked myself mostly out of view.

We'll find a way, Zephyr said. *And in the meantime, we'll keep protecting other mythicals and growing stronger. We've never deliberately killed anyone. At some point, the truth will speak for itself.*

And what if it doesn't? What if those people down there hate us forever?

All leaders are misunderstood and hated by some. Once someone has been blinded to the truth, it takes a lot for them to wake up. We can't let that stop us or make us any less compassionate. They need our care all the more. They've had their perspective warped so badly by lies that they're willing to die for the wrong thing. Zephyr's words were full of sadness, and I didn't doubt that he was talking as much from memory as giving his own advice on how to proceed.

More and more of his genetic memories had unlocked over the last few months, his body now almost fully mature. Sometimes the memories made him excited about stuff we could try, but more often than not, they were things like this, memories of the human race being less than awesome.

I couldn't help him stop having those memories surface, but I could help him make new happier ones.

Pizza? I offered. *And then a fly over the sea for a bit?*

Sounds perfect, he replied, grinning as he did.

"Enjoy whatever you two are scheming. Just make sure you're back before it's too late," Minsheng called as we both made for the stairs into the rest of the building.

"Always," I called back, reminding myself that the part-dwarven man was just showing he cared for Zephyr and me.

We found his sister Daisy in the kitchen, making a round of drinks. Chris was with her. The part gnome was our tech expert and someone who had helped us with our schemes on more than one occasion.

As I entered, Daisy pointed at the oven and the set of pizzas already in it.

"You two always have those on a Friday," she said without even looking at me.

I chuckled and noticed they were almost ready.

"If I had any money, I'd give you a raise," I said as I plonked myself down on a chair. Chris laughed and stirred sugar into his tea.

"I take it that the organization still isn't paying you, then?" he asked as he moved to a laptop sitting on the side and tapped on it.

"Nope. Something about not getting to approve what I'm up to in advance." I grimaced as I spoke, not liking the idea of a group of people I didn't know very well or agree with having that kind of authority over my actions. It didn't solve my money issues to bump heads with them, however.

Before I could ask both Chris and Daisy how they were doing and if the dojo had been busy the last hour or so, a chanting started up from outside again.

"No magic, no way. Only humans here to stay."

They repeated it several times, getting louder. Daisy sighed and shook her head before taking the drinks she'd made away on a tray.

"Well, it was nice and quiet while it lasted," Chris said, picking up his laptop in one hand and his mug of tea in the other. "One day they'll give up, I'm sure."

With that, the part gnome left as well, and only Zephyr and I remained.

Why don't we eat and get out of here? Zephyr said into my head, the oven timer beeping to let us know the pizza was done only seconds later.

There were no arguments from me. I'd had enough of being cooped up already. We wolfed down the food, Zephyr able to eat his straight out of the oven. It took me a little longer, but I grabbed my final slice and followed him back up the building, heading through the dojo's changing area to get up onto the roof.

I found Erlan near the changing area at a large table, also tapping away on a laptop, Emily not far from him. The two of them shared headphones as they listened to a video on the screen.

Grinning at the education the pair were giving each other, I let them be. We'd rescued Emily, a half-elf, from a compound of Jacob's a few months earlier, and she'd instantly taken a liking to Erlan, a full-blooded elf who'd grown up in the Sanctuary before bonding with one of the fire salamanders we'd rescued when we were first on the run in LA.

They had a lot to teach each other about the world and their heritages respectively.

This time as we went up onto the roof and emerged into the construction area, I spotted Crawley, Emily's mother, standing near a window and looking up at the stars.

"I used to take for granted how often I could look up at the sky in peace," the ex-agent said as we came closer.

"Ditto," I replied. "My offer to drop you and Emily off somewhere else still stands, however. You're welcome here, but you could probably start again pretty much anywhere."

"I know, but Emily wants to know who she truly is, and Erlan is helping her work it out. I've only ever wanted what was best for her."

I nodded, not responding in words. Although I hadn't agreed with all of Crawley's actions and what she'd done to other mythicals just to protect her own daughter, I understood it. She'd believed there was no other way to keep Emily safe.

In retrospect, I wasn't sure she was wrong about that either. All the actions I'd taken since finding out I was an elf and had a dragon of my own hadn't exactly led to much in the way of safety.

This is better than the last life I remember, Zephyr projected at me before nudging me with his head. *I'm no longer alone.*

Not alone is definitely better, I replied, thinking how lonely I'd been before I'd found him and we bonded. Although life was hard right now, I didn't think I'd change anything that had started me on this path.

I glanced at him. *Ready?*

Always.

As one, we leaped into the air, Zephyr using his powerful wings while I took control of the air around me and used it to jet me in the direction I wanted to go.

We weren't very high before Zephyr came closer and I settled onto his back. It was a move we'd practiced and performed so many times it was now entirely natural.

While we flew, I relaxed, the familiar way the moonlight glinted off his bronze scales helping me calm down and focus on nothing but the here and now. This was my favorite place in the whole world.

Flying above LA on Zephyr's back with the ocean ahead of us and the city below made me feel less cooped up. The lights had come on everywhere and cars rushed around the streets, forming an elaborate dance.

In its own manmade way, LA was beautiful. And it contrasted with the glittering reflection of the night sky on the ocean beyond.

I sighed as I thought about how little others appreciated it. This was our little part of heaven on earth, and so many never got to see it the way we did.

They'd all want dragons if they knew, Zephyr said.

A laugh escaped me at the idea.

I'm not sure you'd be able to have enough babies to satisfy them all.

Last I checked, it wasn't the male who had the babies.

My eyes went wide as I realized what we were discussing. My cheeks went hot, and I heard Zephyr chuckle. Although we'd talked briefly about how we felt toward each other once, we'd said no more, and well, he was a dragon and I was human.

You know I'll be able to take human form soon, right? he asked a moment later.

So I've been told. It seems a little strange, though. You're a dragon in my mind.

Even in human form, I won't look entirely human. Don't worry. You'll be able to tell I'm a dragon still.

I was wondering what he meant by that when he dived down toward the water and forced me to not only grip tighter but take control of the air around me and form an aerodynamic barrier around me. It took me a while to form it, and by the time I was done, he'd pulled up again, but it meant he could now test a few limits, as we did every evening.

First, Zephyr flew out across the sea as fast as he thought I could go without getting hurt or losing my grip on his back. Slowly we then pushed harder while I adjusted what I was doing and tried to find a way to make it even easier on myself.

Not only was it good exercise for Zephyr to fly so fast for a while, but it also gave me a chance to practice with him. Once we'd done that, it was time for more acrobatics. He looped and rolled almost as if he was trying to dislodge me from his back.

Left roll, he sent into my head so I could prepare for the move. My response was almost entirely instinctive now as I pushed with the air to keep me on his back and also moved some to help him roll even tighter and not lose any height.

Back loop, came the next command, and I tightened my grip as I pushed the air up against my torso to keep me pinned against his back.

By the time he'd performed a few more moves, I was beginning to feel a little sick. As soon as Zephyr noticed, he stopped and gently banked, coming low over the water and brushing the surface with the tips of his wings.

He angled the contact in just the right way that the spray it caused arced up and straight into me. I laughed at the shower, the water cold but forced into a relatively fine mist.

It made me feel better instantly, and then Zephyr slowed and lifted back up a little.

LA was now ahead of us, and I found myself sighing and wishing it was a friendlier place once more. We had our work cut out for us if we were going to stop Jacobs spreading lies about us, and find our place among humanity, however.

One day at a time, Zephyr reminded me.

One day at a time, I agreed. After all, it was all we could really do.

CHAPTER TWO

We were coming back toward the beach, and I was about to ask Zephyr to land at our favorite spot when I noticed there was a lot of activity and splashing in the water several hundred yards farther up.

I watched as Zephyr flew closer to the shore and tried to work out what was happening. Although the beach wasn't usually perfectly quiet at this time of night, there weren't usually so many people in one place.

As we neared, Zephyr altered his course to allow us to get a better look as if he'd read my mind and my desire to know what was going on. I quickly noticed that the people on the shore were carrying baseball bats and other household items like they were weapons, herding the people in the water together and back despite how far they already were into the sea.

Not needing me to tell him to help, Zephyr flew even closer until it was clear that the three people in the water were mythicals, what looked like a couple of dwarves, or gnomes, and possibly an elf. They had a couple of creatures with them, one on a shoulder and another in the elf's arms.

Land between the groups, I thought, knowing Zephyr would hear me.

Already on it, he replied, the seriousness and barely restrained anger in his thoughts enough to put me on edge even if I hadn't also been beginning to feel a similar emotion.

The humans before us looked like they were trying to drown the mythicals. But they weren't going to succeed on my watch.

As Zephyr got closer, I pushed up off his back and flipped backward so I was behind him and the mythicals as he flew over the top and landed on the shore.

There were screams from the humans, and even the mythicals let out yelps and pointed up. I came lower, off to one side so the air I was jetting out to stay in the air didn't cover them in water.

"Get to shore behind Zephyr and I'll make sure you come to no harm," I called over to them.

"Zephyr?" the elf called back. "Are you Aella?"

"Yes," I replied, but I was no longer looking at the mythicals in the water. They weren't yet deep enough that they couldn't touch the bottom and none of them appeared to be struggling. Now Zephyr stood on the shore in front of them, his body acting as a barrier between them and the humans, they were already wading back out.

I flew over and landed near Zephyr's tail as he turned slightly.

The humans immediately stared at me, and the central-most one of the group of seven took a step closer, lifting the baseball bat he carried.

"Get off our beach, scum. And take your pet lizard with you. We don't want your kind here in our city."

"Last I checked this beach was for all the residents of LA and we can be here all we want," I replied. "I suggest you find another section of it if you have a problem with me and Zephyr."

"Or what? You're going to kill us like you did those soldiers you ambushed? You deserve to go to hell just like others of your kind."

"I didn't kill any soldiers that day, and even if I had, they were on their way to murder harmless mythicals just for existing," I snapped, feeling my body tense as I stepped forward.

Aella, calm, Zephyr's voice commanded, almost booming through all my other thoughts and feelings like a tidal wave of sense. Immediately I relaxed and took a deep breath. I couldn't let my anger get the better of me. I couldn't afford to make a mistake like that.

"Go on, inhuman scum, attack us. Show us how little respect you have for human life," one of the girls to the left yelled.

I looked her way and immediately noticed the cell she was holding up as if she was filming me and Zephyr as well as the mythicals behind.

"I'm not going to attack anyone, but I will defend the mythicals you appear to be attempting to drown." As I spoke, I threw up a barrier with my mind. While none of the young humans in front of me looked as if they had guns, I wasn't going to take any chances.

"They deserve to die," another one of them yelled.

"You can join them," the leader said.

"No. If they've broken any laws, then feel free to report them to the cops. I'll even keep them here until they arrive. But if this is what it looks like, your mistaken hate getting the better of your judgment, then I and they will be leaving. Hopefully, with us somewhere else, it will give you all the chance to calm down and think more clearly again."

"Mistaken hate. Is that what you think this is?" The baseball bat holder lifted it again. "Drown, bitch. You killed good men."

He rushed forward and swung the bat, but I merely lifted a hand and forced the air back on the tip, knocking it out of his hands. It flew up in the air, but before it could spin in the wrong direction and hit the girl filming, I blasted it with air again and sent it flying up and over her head. It landed at the top of the beach.

Some of the others rushed the other mythicals again, but Zephyr got in the way and roared. They hesitated and that gave me a chance to act on a larger scale.

Bending down and reaching into the beach with my mind, I took control of it, making it give way beneath the humans, swallowing their legs and then hardening around them to hold them in place.

With that, I backed up out of reach and watched them try to struggle themselves free. It wasn't going to hold them for long since my bond with the earthen elements was still far weaker than my bond with the air, but it was enough for me to motion to the other mythicals to get on Zephyr's back.

They looked at me, then the elf had the sense to begin

climbing up. The shorter two soon followed, their creatures also running up Zephyr's scales to safety.

While they climbed, I looked for the girl with the camera trained on me and strode closer before crouching down so I was in the shot.

"I've never wanted to harm anyone, but I'll say what I always do. I will defend myself and those like me. Let us live in peace, and we'll be no trouble to anyone. The choice is humanity's."

With that, I stepped back and checked Zephyr had everyone.

We're good to go, Zephyr said before his powerful wings lifted him into the air with a single downbeat. It picked up sand and small stones and flicked them toward the humans and me, but I quickly stopped them, using both my abilities at once, and made them fall back to the beach.

Once that was done, I looked at the camera again.

"Leave us in peace," I said again before also jetting myself upward and into the air after Zephyr. I didn't look back to see if the camera continued to follow me, but I heard the insults the group continued to hurl.

I sighed as I tried to remember the last good interaction I'd had with a full human who didn't know me and who decided I was okay, like Lyra, who had offered to hide Zephyr and me when he had been the size of a cat. Or my sensei from my martial arts lessons before I even knew I wasn't human either.

It had been a long time ago. And all because Jacobs had decided to paint me as a murderer rather than accept that the world knew about mythicals now.

Back to the warehouse, I suggested to Zephyr as I caught

up with him and flew overhead to keep an eye on the three mythicals he carried. I used the air to give him more lift without his having to work so hard. He wasn't used to carrying so many people, and despite his being strong enough and large enough now, I felt it was only right that I helped.

It didn't take us long to get back to the warehouse. Zephyr carefully landed with all the mythicals safely still in place. I touched down beside him, taking care again not to blast anyone with air while I slowed and stopped.

The three new arrivals and their animal companions slid down his side until they were standing, bedraggled and wide-eyed, in the middle of the building site.

"You'll have to forgive the mess," I said. "We're adding some bedrooms for the mythicals we've got living here already."

None of them replied, but Daisy appeared a moment later and instantly hurried over.

"Oh my, you must all be so cold," she said, ushering the shell-shocked trio toward the stairs.

As she did, I got the impression she'd been expecting us, towels and hot drinks to hand at the bottom of the stairs, Minsheng and Chris also standing there waiting.

I walked over to Minsheng but before I could open my mouth to ask questions, Chris lifted his laptop and showed me a video already on social media of the exchange on the beach. The girl hadn't just been filming, she'd been live-streaming everything.

"All things considered, you handled it pretty well," Minsheng said as I frowned. "But it appears as if it's not enough to sway some minds."

"You never convince everyone," Zephyr replied for me, the room going silent as he did. It was rare for him to speak, and when he did, people knew he meant what he was saying. "Someone will always remain convinced they're right and you're evil. But they become the minority, and with time there are less people to fuel their opinions."

"In the world of the internet, it's a lot easier for someone like that to find someone else and have them fuel each other, but Zephyr's right," Daisy said. "Eventually good wins out."

I nodded, hoping they were all right. That in time this would all be over and easier.

"What now?" the elf asked, his masculine voice still somehow soft. "We cannot go back to our lives. So many treat us badly."

I looked over the three we'd rescued, each one of them now wrapped in a towel and holding a hot drink of some kind. It looked like the dwarven pair were related, possibly even twins, the girl a less hairy version of the boy. The male elf had an animal I'd never seen before on his lap, but it appeared to be shy and curled up under the blanket as much as possible.

On the dwarven woman's shoulder was a bird. It wasn't one I recognized, but it had a beautiful purple and red plumage.

"I would offer you a home here, but I don't think it's going to be much safer, and right now we don't have a lot of space," I said a moment later. "There is the Sanctuary, however. I could take you there myself. Make sure nothing happens to you."

"What's the Sanctuary?"

"It's a place where mythicals are safe. A small city with many mythicals and creatures. Protected and hidden, only those with an orb and mythical DNA can find it."

"That sounds amazing," the female dwarf said. "Are there others who've come from the human world?"

"Some," I replied. "More so in the last few months. They're very welcoming either way."

I sighed as they looked eager and excited, the distraught behavior melting under the hope of a new future somewhere better suited for them. Despite understanding their desire to go somewhere safer, I felt a little jealous of the Sanctuary's appeal. I had wanted to be a haven for so many of my kind. But I seemed to be on some kind of front line instead.

"Let me gather some gear and I'll take you there as soon as possible. It's probably best we head out while it's still dark, so I won't be more than a few minutes." I nodded to Minsheng as he held out some snack bars and a bottle of water.

Having my Shishou practically read my mind was a definite plus, but I needed something to carry it in. I had a feeling I was going to need my hands free.

Over the months I'd been on the run and traveling back and forth I'd acquired a few packs, so I hurried to my room to dig out one I currently didn't have anything in.

It was only as I was looking through the bottom of the wardrobe I now had that I noticed a strange package. I'd seen it before but forgotten all about it. Someone had tidied it away for me at some point and I'd not seen it again until now.

Knowing I was keeping the others waiting but feeling like it was important to finally find out what was inside, I sat down on the end of the large bed I shared with Zephyr. The package was wrapped in leather. Sierrathen had given it to me the first time I'd visited the Sanctuary.

I'd left the city to stop an agent discovering their location, and right before I said my final goodbye, one of the councilors had come to the border to give me this. Because of the impending threat I'd not been able to open it, instead shoving it in the bottom of a pack and forgetting about it entirely.

Zephyr came into the room, possibly sensing the change in my thoughts and behavior, and sat himself down next to me as I pulled back the flap and revealed the contents.

Two tan, leather bracers sat in the middle, two interwoven trees depicted on each.

"These are beautiful," I said aloud, feeling my skin tingle as I touched them. Instinctively I seemed to know they were magic, just like Tuviel's necklace now resting against my skin, which strengthened the bond I had with Zephyr.

They were Laeroth's. I recognize them, Zephyr said into my head. *And, yes. They're also magical.*

Wasn't Laeroth the great earth elf, Tuviel's counterpart?

Yes. He was. And only a great earth elf will be able to wear them and have them work.

Like the necklace, I replied, continuing Zephyr's thought. I slipped my arm through the middle of one and pulled the ties to fix it in place. Almost as if it had a mind of its own, it continued to tighten until it fit perfectly against my arm.

It tingled for just a moment before fading to a background pleasant warmth.

Quickly I put the second on as well, finding it also fitted itself to me and warmed to my skin.

I blinked, not sure I could speak or process how it made me feel. Suddenly I was aware of the plant I had in a pot on my shelf. I could feel it and how alive and capable it was. The strength in it and the potential to be so much more.

It was only a couple of feet tall as it was, and I'd had to repot it twice. Not something that had come naturally to me, but the water master at the Sanctuary had given it to me and told me to practice.

Initially I'd been trying to get the water out of the soil, but instead I'd somehow grown one of the most difficult plants known to the mythical races.

Getting up, I went over to it and reached out. The plant seemed to lean into my hand, and I reached for it with my mind as I had other plants in battle and tried to encourage it to grow some more. Within seconds it was two inches taller and the pot was dry.

Not wanting to kill it, I stopped and immediately reached for the glass of water I'd left nearby the night before. I poured some in and waited until I could sense the roots finding it and starting to suck up the life-giving liquid.

Then I backed off and exhaled to calm my racing heart.

Zephyr came closer and leaned his head against mine.

You're growing more powerful. I think I can feel the plant now as well. Through you. Like it's an extension of your body.

As if you could control it as well?

No idea, Zephyr replied. *But we've got time to find out. We should set off to the Sanctuary before it gets any later.*

I nodded and grabbed a jacket, making sure it covered the bracers. I wasn't ready to answer questions about them yet, and they stood out.

CHAPTER THREE

Moving on the power of the wind and trying to glide a little, I flew alongside Zephyr.

We were just over halfway between LA and the Sanctuary, our three mythical companions riding on Zephyr's back so we could move quickly and quietly over the unsuspecting human population.

I had an orb with me, but we barely needed it. The Sanctuary had relocated to a spot Ronan and I had found for them a few months earlier and had been able to stay safe and hidden there without trouble since. It was still useful, however. I wasn't taking any chances in making sure the three mythicals we'd rescued and their animal companions got to the Sanctuary safely.

How are you doing? I asked Zephyr when I noticed him dip a little and take a lower path, appearing to be trying to rest his wings while gliding as well.

Getting tired. We should look for a good spot to rest. These three are a lot heavier than you, and they don't help the way you can.

I doubt they know how to do magic, or even know they can, I thought as I pushed a little farther ahead and tried to look for a place that would accommodate and hide us for a bit. It was almost entirely pointless for me to do it in the dark, Zephyr the one with the good eyesight, but I noticed mine had been improving. It was better than a human's now.

On top of that, I soon noticed I could reach out for the plants below. I found a set of woods off to our right with a clearing not too far in, bushes, grasses and even flowers there for me to connect to.

Over this way, I suggested and started flying in that direction. As I got closer, I could see that I'd felt the terrain correctly and we landed in the middle of the woods, the clearing just wide enough Zephyr could stretch his wings out without clipping anything. He'd have a little difficulty flying up and out again, but I could help if needed.

As I landed I looked around, aware the forest felt so alive around me. It was more than a little strange, but it felt right, the way flying did.

"We'll rest here for a few minutes and then go the rest of the way. We're over halfway there now."

"That was amazing," the female dwarf said, a grin on her face. "You're so lucky to get to do that whenever you want."

I smiled and nodded, definitely aware of the special moments I'd had flying through the air. Almost no one else ever got to do anything so cool.

With everyone on solid ground, we broke out the snacks and drinks and I chowed down, offering Zephyr some of my snack bars.

Keep them. You'll probably need them, and I can hunt something later.

I didn't need any persuading. Having more snacks to myself after using my powers so much was a definite plus. Using magic cost a lot of energy although I could control it far more efficiently than when I'd begun the previous year. It still used calories like crazy. I was almost always hungry.

While the others were resting and Zephyr was keeping guard, I moved to the edge of the clearing, reaching for the trees. It was almost as if I couldn't help it, my feet moving forward of their own accord.

What can you feel? Zephyr asked a moment later, lifting his head and fixing his gaze on me as I looked back his way.

Not sure. Just...something. There's a plant or tree that's...stronger, I thought as I tried to describe the tug I was feeling to go into the woods.

Be careful.

Always. And I don't think it's far away.

No sooner had I thought this than I felt whatever it was move closer, almost as if it was hopping toward me, as aware of my presence as I was of it. What was it? Last I'd been aware, plants couldn't move, let alone bounce.

I took another step toward the clearing and crouched, the shape of the life I felt getting clearer as it came nearer.

When it was still about thirty feet away I spotted it. A small toadstool or mushroom-like creature no bigger than the palm of my hand. It felt like a plant, but I watched as it slowed and stopped near the base of a tree, its small eyes blinking up at me briefly.

"Hello, there," I said gently, noticing Zephyr stand again at my words.

He walked closer as the mushroom tipped its hat-like top to one side and studied me.

"I won't hurt you. I'm an elf," I added, reaching out my hand. "I can feel you."

The creature reached out a twig-thin arm that split into three on the end, like two fingers and a thumb. It was cute, with its big eyes and wide mushroom top above the smallest face I'd ever seen.

Slowly it shuffled closer.

"Sen," it said with a squeak as it came closer and tapped the part of the stalk that seemed to be its chest or torso.

"Aella," I replied, tapping myself as well. It hopped and scuttled on two legs that divided out of the stalk and seemed to have root-like ends. They were clearly strong, often bouncing the small creature over obstacles so he or she didn't have to go around them.

I smiled at the strange way of moving until it was only a couple of feet away from me, just in the shadows of the forest. It finally noticed Zephyr and the others and its eyes grew even wider.

"Zephyr," I said, pointing at the dragon. "Friend."

It moved cautiously closer as Zephyr deliberately sat down again.

I believe that's a dryad of a sort, he said into my head as I reached for it with my mind again. *A wood fairy or wood sprite are also accurate names for it. The myconid variety.*

Cool. It's cute.

And powerful. Don't underestimate it.

Noted. It seems friendly though.

Yes. They're normally very shy creatures, especially since humans have expanded so much across the world. They don't usually come out to meet people.

I think it was drawn to me as I was drawn to it, I explained as it turned its attention on me again.

She, I think, Zephyr added a moment later.

Deciding to use the trick I had when making friends with Zephyr a long time ago, I blinked slowly a couple of times, and stayed very still.

"Sen Sen," it said as it came even closer, inspecting my outstretched hand.

I didn't dare move, something about the moment making my heart race. This creature was something special and I felt like I wanted to pick it up and take it with me, but I didn't dare.

Was this what the bracers had changed? Had they made me more aware of creatures like this in the same way the necklace Tuviel had worn had made me more aware of Zephyr?

With no way to know, I could only wait as Sen shuffled closer and closer. I didn't want to scare her.

She inched nearer a bit at a time, reaching out until her hand touched the end of one of my fingers. There was a flash of bright light, and I felt something leave me and connect with the creature. The myconid's mind opened up in a mass of pictures and feelings, the energy that came with it making my heart stop for a moment.

Zephyr stood as I met Sen's gaze, my mouth wide open.

I was pretty sure I'd just bonded with her.

You did. Zephyr's words came into my head.

Bond, Sen added in a moment later before nodding.

But how? I'm already bonded to Zephyr.

She shrugged, and that moved the cup of the mushroom more than any other part of her.

It must be your recent ability to use earth magic as well, Zephyr said, also coming closer and leaning down near the small mushroom. Sen reached out and touched the very end of his snout with her tiny hand, the difference in their sizes almost alarming.

"Did something epic just happen?" the elf asked as he also dared to come closer.

"Yes," I said as I stood, my mind struggling to catch up. "This little myconid and I have just bonded. Elves can bond with mythical creatures sometimes."

"But I thought you were bonded with Zephyr," the dwarf girl said. I nodded.

"Yeah. I appear to now be bonded with Sen here too."

I found myself slowly grinning as I spoke. It was a crazy thing, but if anything had been confirmation that I might have DNA in me from all the different great elves, this was it. Slowly I bent again and offered to pick up the tiny wood sprite. There was no way I was leaving it behind, and that meant I had to find somewhere safe for it to ride with us while we flew.

While I held out my hand again, I thought comforting thoughts, worried that she wouldn't want to leave her home, but a grin spread across her face and she leaped into my palm.

Fly? she asked, her words having a deep tone in contrast to the high-pitched introduction she'd given me vocally.

Fly, I thought in reply before hearing Zephyr chuckle.

28

But we need to find you somewhere safe. It will be fast. I don't want you to get hurt.

Sen not hurt, she said as she tilted her head to the side and studied me again. A moment later she was running up my arm, using both her hands and feet to grip onto the jacket. Within seconds she was near my shoulder, where she stopped.

I held very still, worried I might knock her off if I wasn't careful, but she seemed to be able to grip much more tightly than I'd given her credit for. She swung over toward the jacket opening and slipped into it, right above the zipper.

She burrowed in, not that far below my neck, and settled down.

Sen safe, she said a moment later.

I looked up to see Zephyr's mouth open in a wide toothy grin. No doubt I looked more than a little strange, but at the same time, I was over the moon and blown away. I'd bonded with a second mythical.

Aware I was being stared at by the companions we were escorting to the Sanctuary, I forced myself to focus on why we were originally out here. They still needed to get somewhere safe. I was also now really excited to go find the Sanctuary's earth master.

I didn't doubt that he'd be super excited about hearing of this new development. As would the water master, who had set me down this path in the first place.

After encouraging the mythicals back onto Zephyr's back and checking the dragon was comfortable with such a heavy load, I reached out to control more air and used it to help Zephyr lift and get up into the air again.

Despite us working together, he still clipped the tops of some of the trees but he was soon far above them, his powerful wings able to bear him and his burdens into the night sky.

Ready? I asked my new companion, worried that what was about to happen would be a huge shock to her.

Sen safe, the creature replied.

I took a deep breath and as controlled and gently as I could I lifted myself up into the air, still just about able to see Zephyr as I followed him into the sky.

Although he was a dark mass in a cloudy night sky, I could sense him as well and knew where to head. For now my focus was on the creature tucked in the top of my jacket.

Naturally, I formed air around myself to make my shape more aerodynamic, and it appeared to shield Sen as well but let her get a good view.

Sen still safe? I thought as we got higher and I shifted forward to fly forward instead of just up.

Sen fly. Sen like, she replied a moment later.

Emboldened by her approval and delight, I pushed a little harder. We'd dropped behind Zephyr while I was being so cautious but I soon started to catch up again and flew alongside him. I could feel the excitement Sen was projecting in a way I didn't usually feel Zephyr's emotions.

While like this, I could also marvel at the differences in my bond with the myconid. Although she could speak, her thoughts and feelings seemed to come across more in images with sensations and something a bit like a cross between emotions and colors.

It was strange and very different to Zephyr's way of communicating with me, but I warmed to it just as quickly.

I can feel it too. Not as strongly as you can, but I'm aware of her, Zephyr said a moment later.

Can you hear her thoughts too?

Only when she actively sends them to both of us, I think. I've only heard her twice. Zephyr seemed to sigh and underneath the purplish excitement and delight Sen was projecting I got the hint of something else, something Zephyr was feeling.

You okay?

Fine, Zephyr replied, but there was a bite to it that suggested otherwise. I found myself wondering what had made him snappy, but I knew he could hear me wondering and he didn't say anything.

What's wrong? I asked a short while later, detecting a hint of discomfort and aware Sen was also beginning to pick up on it.

I caught half snippets of thoughts and emotions as Zephyr moved through them. It was almost as if he was trying to shield them from me but not quite managing it. He seemed both cross at himself and frustrated about something. And under it all lay an anxiety I'd never felt from him before. Normally he was calm, far calmer than I was.

Are you jealous? I asked a moment later. *Or worried that this changes anything between us?*

Both. He sighed. *Definitely both. You're now bonded with another in a way that I thought was unique to us. Something that made us...*

Special. It wasn't the exact word but it finished Zephyr's sentence. It left out a huge amount of feelings we'd not spoken about much. I cared about Zephyr far deeper and more completely than I'd ever cared about anyone before.

I love you. Zephyr's voice boomed, my own mind echoing the words that had come out of the blue. I thought I'd be shocked—after all, he was a dragon—but in truth he was also mine in every way and I'd known it for some time.

I love you too, I thought back.

The words had never come so easily, and I felt them settle some of the noise in Zephyr's head. I meant them with every fiber of my being. I was in love with Zephyr. A dragon. And it was both so completely weird but so completely right.

CHAPTER FOUR

As the Sanctuary came into view I felt relieved. This had felt like a long journey despite the exciting moment in the middle and the revelation from Zephyr and I about how we felt.

With the extra mythicals under our care, we'd had to be careful, and a couple of times we'd even flown around some civilized areas that were beginning to wake up.

The sky had been getting brighter before we reached the border of the mythical haven, and I'd begun to grow more than a little concerned that we'd be spotted before we could get there.

Thankfully we'd been able to stick to uninhabited areas and no one had seen us. At least no one who made themselves obvious or attacked. That was good enough.

We landed again still a little way out from the shield and illusion barrier that protected the Sanctuary from the humans nearby, and our companions slid off Zephyr's back once more. I glanced his way as I walked forward, knowing that only he and I could see the beautiful city ahead.

This one was in the mountains, and although some of it was in a cave network below the surface of the Rockies, the rest was built above and onto the solid foundation.

The Sanctuary contained several other earth elves, and they had come together to create yet another stunning set of dwellings formed from plants and trees, and this time even the rock around had been moved and molded. I couldn't wait to reach the edge and see the reactions of those around me.

Sen okay? I asked, feeling the creature shift out of my jacket.

Sen see better, she replied as she climbed up onto my shoulder and stood there, holding onto the lock of hair tucked behind my ear. It felt a little strange but equally right in its own way.

Just as I'd done the first time I'd gone toward the Sanctuary, the other mythicals sped up, drawn onward and upward along the path until they finally reached the barrier and stepped beyond it.

All three of them stopped and gaped as Zephyr came up close to my side to get past some of the nearby trees.

We'd only taken a couple more steps when a gnome jumped down from another tree ahead.

"Hello," he said. "And welcome to the Sanctuary. He nodded at me, a familiar patrol guard, but his focus quickly returned to the three new visitors with me.

"I'll take them to the new arrivals area and get them settled in," I said. "Can you let the council know I'm here but that there's nothing major to report since my last visit? I'll be with one of the masters after that."

"Consider it done. I assume no trouble comes on your tail this time?"

"No. None that I'm aware of. We flew around anyone who might see us," I said as he climbed up a thin rope and got back onto the small wooden platform hidden in his tree.

I carried onward, not giving anyone any more time to take it in. As much as I didn't want to ruin their first impression, I was tired and I didn't doubt that they were as well.

With the sun coming up I felt fairly awake right now, but I wanted to get everything I had to do out of the way and then get back to the dojo and my friends.

Zephyr walked along beside me, towering over me and beginning to cast a shadow in the morning light. I reached out a hand and placed it on his shoulder, having to reach up almost as high as I could.

Although he wouldn't grow very much now, almost at full size, larger than the average car and solid to go with it, I still remembered the day he'd hatched, the size of a cat. It had been a long time since he was small enough to carry around inside the pack on my back.

It wasn't long before someone came out of the city to greet us, A familiar elf and a centaur walking side by side.

"Hello, Seth. Hello, Lorcan," I said to each of them in turn. I noticed Seth's eyes flick to the dryad on my shoulder. He lifted an eyebrow, but he made no comment yet. For him, it was restrained.

"We've brought these three here to stay for a while," I continued when no one else spoke. "I hope you've got some space for them."

"All mythicals are welcome here," Lorcan replied. "And I see you have one of the rare wood sprites with you. If she would also like to stay, I know there are a couple of others with us now."

"I have a feeling that she'll be sticking with me," I replied, caught off guard and not sure how to bring up the bonding.

Seth hadn't been very accommodating when he'd found out I'd bonded with Zephyr when, in his opinion, I wasn't a full-blooded elf with any right to be bonded at all. I didn't doubt that the elf was going to hate finding out I was now bonded with two mythicals.

Lorcan studied me, then dipped his head and turned to Seth.

"We'll continue our conversation later, my friend. Can you take our new guests to the new arrivals center and see they're given food and a place to rest? No doubt they will be tired by now. I should continue my duty as commander of the guard and ascertain the current situation in the human world."

"Thank you," I said, as much to Seth as Lorcan. I briefly said goodbye to the mythicals as they went with their elf guide and moved deeper into the city. Lorcan walked off to one side, and Zephyr and I fell in beside him. We found a good spot out of the way and under the shade of a large tree to stop and sit.

Within seconds I was telling him what had happened and why I'd brought the three of them to the city, and then I answered his questions, being as honest as I could while still being hopeful that one day humanity would become more accepting of all mythicals.

"And this myconid?" Lorcan asked. "She seems very at home with you for a creature you met on the way. If it were possible, I'd say you've bonded with her."

I gulped. It wasn't a good start if Lorcan didn't think it possible and was assuming it was something else already.

He studied me once more.

"Has the impossible happened?" he asked a moment later.

"I believe so. We believe so." I looked to Zephyr as I spoke the last bit.

"Then you truly..." Lorcan trailed off, lowering his head. "It is not my place to speak of it, but I must inform the council. I hope you understand, but this changes things. I hope I can trust that you'll be willing to stay until they've had time to prepare a bonding ceremony for you. They will want to test the bond, I'm sure."

I frowned, not sure how to answer such a statement. Lorcan's words drew a complicated mix of emotions to the surface.

On one hand I'd once lamented the lack of bonding ceremony I'd received for bonding with Zephyr and longed to have the opportunity, but on the other hand I wasn't sure I wanted one for only one of my bonds. It wasn't fair to Zephyr. Despite all that, I had a feeling I wasn't intended to have much choice about it.

As Lorcan got to his feet again and trotted off to the center of the Sanctuary, I didn't move. What did I do now?

It's best to do it, Zephyr said into my head, his voice both resigned and sad.

I don't want this to hurt you, I replied. *We bonded first and we had no ceremony.*

And maybe we should have asked for one. But I will be fine. We'll adjust. Come, let us find the earth master and tell him. His inevitable excitement might be good for all of us.

Before Zephyr could stand, I leaned into him and sighed. Once more, I was starting to get the feeling that others were going to try and dictate my future to me. I could only hope that wasn't true. Either way, Zephyr was right. Excitement from someone we respected and liked might help.

As Zephyr got up, I moved closer again, resting my hand on him and walking, now three of us. I wasn't sure how the future was going to look, but we would need to find a new balance and I was committed to both creatures now bonded with me.

We found the earth master in a strange building that had the mountain as its back but opened to the sky on one half. It appeared to be formed of living trees, foliage covering the walls and tree limbs becoming beams to support the roof.

"Aella," Orthelo said as soon as he spotted me, a bird of some kind eating seed out of his hand. Another sat on his shoulder, looking at me. It was small, with bright red plumage.

"Is that the phoenix?" I asked, taking in the small bird.

"It is. It hatched not long after you came, but it's still vulnerable and needs constant care for now. I think it's going well to begin with, even if I'm not getting as much sleep right now."

The earth master grinned and then looked my way, the seed in his hand now gone and the bird he'd been feeding flying off.

"I see you have a new creature with you too. Are you bringing her to me to look after?"

I grinned slightly at everyone thinking she was also in need of the Sanctuary, but I shook my head.

Orthelo came closer and inspected the dryad on my shoulder. As he did, I glanced sideways at Sen to make sure she was okay with the close proximity. A smile was fixed on her face, and she reached out the hand that wasn't holding my hair and gently touched his finger, almost as if this was how she greeted people.

"She's a rare sight and beautiful. Has she said anything?" Orthelo asked, his eyes alight with genuine curiosity and happiness at being introduced to a new mythical.

"Sen," I replied. "Her name's Sen, and I believe I've just bonded with her."

"You..." his eyes went even wider and then he clapped his hands in delight. "Oh, my dear child. You've bonded with an earth creature as well? This is marvelous news. Have you told anyone else? What a discovery! What a breakthrough, and during this troubled time. It..."

Orthelo trailed off as he took hold of both my arms and studied me.

"Yes. Yes. It is happening. Ruehnar was right. You're her. Oh my. I barely dared to hope I'd ever see these days."

His eyes shone with a strange light, then he leaned forward and kissed my forehead.

I lifted my eyebrows but kept still, puzzled by this behavior.

"You're the second person to imply something important has just happened, but I'm none the wiser," I eventually said.

"Forgive me, forgive me. I'm merely an excited old elf who has waited a long time to meet a young one of your power and skill. There have been many to dream of this, to hope for this. But I don't know how much is mine to say." Orthelo backed off a little, but he still smiled in a joyous fashion that was so pure I couldn't help but feel better for it.

"I think I'm going to insist you enlighten us. Zephyr and I, and now Sen, are likely to need to know what people are about to expect of us."

"Enlightenment shall definitely be yours as soon as it can be arranged," Sierrathen said from over my shoulder. As one, Zephyr and I turned and he almost caught her with his tail. One of the Sanctuary council members, I was never sure if I was happy to see her, but she appeared to be alone.

"Lorcan informed me," she added by way of an explanation. "And he goes to tell the rest of the council now. I have come to make a request of you. Would you come and perform the bonding ceremony and allow us to right an old wrong while asking for your forgiveness?"

"It depends," I replied, reaching for Zephyr again. "What wrong do you intend to right? And what does a bonding ceremony entail on my part exactly? I saw Erlan's a half a year ago, but I didn't understand all of it. And can it be done with both my bonded mythicals? I have no desire to leave Zephyr out of something when he was my first companion, and for a while, he was the only mythical I knew I could trust and rely on for support."

Sierrathen sighed and I held her gaze as she studied me, prepared to fight for the respect Zephyr and I deserved. I felt Sen crouch and her mushroom top shifted, lifting up. Zephyr lowered his head, and I thought I heard him let out a deep but brief rumble. I could feel similar emotions to my own from both of them, a preparation to stand our ground.

The elven council member looked between us and nodded.

"Let me be clear and speak as plainly as I can. The very wrong I wish to right is the one you've spoken of. To give you and Zephyr the honor of a bonding ceremony. To recognize your strengths and abilities in front of the whole Sanctuary as they should have been the day you arrived. The council didn't know what to make of you when you dropped in on us last year, and many of the residents here still don't."

"That's not exactly my problem, but I appreciate someone finally acknowledging it," I replied.

"Yes, well. I'd like to help show them who you truly are and see if we can change a few minds."

"You, or the council?"

"You've already convinced Lorcan that you're an asset and worth working with, but not all the others can see the path forward yet. *I'm* asking you and *I* alone."

I exhaled, appreciating the honesty but not sure I wanted to truly engage in a PR campaign within the Sanctuary when I was also fighting a PR nightmare in the human world. I'd done nothing wrong but had to fight my way into people's good books from the moment I'd found out I was an elf. I was getting tired of it.

Equally, I was being offered something I'd wanted. A bonding ceremony that recognized what I had with Zephyr as well as allowed me to deepen my bond with Sen. For that reason alone, I was tempted to say yes.

Slowly Zephyr relaxed and then he moved to bring his head close to mine and Sen's.

I think we should do it, he said. *I think we should show them what we're all capable of together already and let them make their own minds up after that.*

It felt as if Sen had heard Zephyr's words as well because she reached out again and placed her small hand on Zephyr's nose and smiled. The warmth flowing between them was quickly apparent and it helped me relax.

Sen like. Sen want ceremony, the dryad replied, ceremony coming out in a strange fashion as if it was a new word for the creature.

"All right," I said aloud. "A double bonding ceremony that recognizes the bond that now exists between all three of us. But if either of them is slighted or favored, or anyone gives me crap for something I both had no control over and never asked for, I'm probably going to take my bonded mythicals with me and leave. I've had enough of being judged for events and situations that were thrust upon me."

"Your requests are understandable," Sierrathen replied. "And I will endeavor to do my best to see them fulfilled. I know the bonding ceremony is considered a very sacred thing. I do not expect any to disrespect the moment."

"They had better not, and you had better do everything you're capable of, because none of what I said was a request. It was a condition. A demand, and nothing less will be acceptable. I'll be treated with respect or I'll stop working with you. It's that simple."

Sierrathen lifted her eyebrows but she inclined her head in the manner the centaurs often did and then she hurried away, her graceful form moving back along the path toward the heart of the Sanctuary.

As the three of us finally relaxed, I heard Orthelo chuckle to himself. I turned to face him. He smiled at me and grew more serious once more.

"It's been a long time since I've seen someone give the council an ultimatum and force them to change when they need it. You've given me two gifts today, Aella, and I am in your debt. The memory of the great elemental elves of old has faded with time, but I feel like I've seen them again today."

I nodded, but I didn't feel entirely satisfied. No one had given me any answers about who they all thought I might be, and I quickly said as much.

"I promise I and the other masters will explain as soon as your bonded ceremony is complete but there is no time now. Will that suffice to abate your rightful desire to understand?"

"It will, for now," I replied before relenting and heading with Orthelo back toward the Sanctuary's heart as well. It seemed we had a bonding ceremony to attend.

CHAPTER FIVE

Surrounded by what looked like the entire city of mythicals and many creatures on top of that, I felt more than a little in the spotlight. We were in the largest cavern I'd ever seen, sunlight reflecting off and through crystals to cast a beautiful glow over the whole area. Here and there, stalactites and stalagmites had met to form natural pillars that appeared to hold the ceiling up, but I could barely take in the beauty of it while everyone was staring at me.

Thankfully, I wasn't alone. I had Zephyr and Sen.

The three of us were standing in a triangle, and it was almost comical with the size differences, but equally, it felt right. I had a feeling that Sen could make up for her small size in various ways, and she didn't seem frightened by the height of everything around her. Of course, I didn't doubt that she was used to something similar, as I'd found her in a forest of tall trees.

"Thank you all for coming," Sierrathen said as the room went quiet and she gained everyone's attention.

I'd spotted Lorcan, Seth, and several others I knew in

the crowds, but some of them came closer now, almost as if they sensed my need to have more support.

"As is normal in the Sanctuary, when an elf bonds with a mythical, we perform the bonding ceremony and both test this bond and celebrate it. It is a special moment that strengthens all of us. For an elf to bond is a sign that we've not been forsaken. That we are still allies. And that bond gives us protection, comfort, and relationship. It brings understanding and compassion and strength and power. It is a symbiotic joining, and it signifies a new beginning for everyone involved."

There was a silence as Sierrathen paused. I took several deep breaths to try and calm my racing heart. I didn't remember Erlan's bonding ceremony having such a speech at the beginning of it, but then, he'd not bonded with two creatures of different elements, and he wasn't being trotted out as some hopeful beacon of the future.

"Aella, Zephyr, and Sen stand before us today as bonded mythicals," Sierrathen continued, motioning to each of us with a hand as she said our names.

There were collective gasps as she included the third one, and people jostled as they tried to get a glimpse of the small mythical standing in her own space on the gleaming cavern floor.

"Yes, you heard me correctly. Aella has bonded with a dragon of the air origin and a dryad of the earth origin, and as most are already aware, displayed an affinity to control both elements." Sierrathen again paused as a ripple of conversation and more gasps spread outwards.

All eyes were back on the three of us again, and I saw Sen shift her body, her mushroom top drooping a little. Zephyr also moved his weight back and forth across his front feet as he'd done when younger and anxious.

I reached for both of them with my mind and projected calm at them despite not fully feeling it myself. Maybe I could help them even if I felt nervous myself.

We've got this licked, Zephyr said a moment later. *Don't worry. Even with the young bond with Sen, we can do anything they'll ask.*

Sen agree.

I found myself smiling at the reassurance they both gave back. There truly was no hiding anything.

"Now, for the first test. The stones," Sierrathen instructed. Someone to her left handed her three and she walked forward, placing them on the ground behind each of us.

Thankfully, this bit was something I had seen before. Erlan had touched his at the same time as Newton and they'd both lit up, confirming the bond. Or something like that. It had made everyone extremely excited and happy if nothing else.

As she returned to her position, I took another deep breath, and then, as one, all three of us turned so we couldn't see each other and touched the stones. Instantly they all lit up, glowing a deep purple that was so bright it almost blinded me.

While my vision adjusted, I stepped back and turned the stone away from me, blocking most of the light coming my way with my hand. As I turned toward the center again, I noticed Zephyr held his in this mouth, and Sen stood atop of hers.

Silence filled the cavern so completely that I could hear water dripping somewhere off behind Sierrathen.

"I've never seen them light up so brightly," she said, her eyes wide as she stared. "Nor so swiftly. And such a beautiful color."

This seemed to break the moment, and as quiet as it had been, it quickly transformed into the complete opposite. I looked around as everyone talked and pointed, Orthelo and the other masters smiling and beginning to clap. Not everyone seemed pleased with my performance, however. Some of the elves gave me dark looks and shook their heads.

I noticed another few mythicals appearing to have an argument, and I was pretty sure the willow-like mythical on the council was among them. It was almost enough to make me fly off with Zephyr and Sen right then and there. This was exactly the sort of disrespect I'd warned Sierrathen I was sick of tolerating.

She stepped forward and cleared her throat.

"Mythicals," she said as loudly as she could. "We may have seen something unexpected that we will need to talk at length, but the bonding ceremony is not yet complete."

I exhaled again, knowing what came next and deciding to give the councilor a chance to convince the rest of the Sanctuary that we were a powerful ally. We had to show that we were powerful and capable of all sorts of control over our magical elements. As soon as I'd known where we were going to be, I'd decided what I wanted to do. It was going to take a fair bit of concentration, however.

As I reached for the air and the earth, I closed my eyes. I felt Sen run to Zephyr as the dragon lowered his head to let the myconid flip and bounce her way onto his neck. Sen moved back as I also ran forward and jumped, rolling and flipping, my abilities helping me somersault onto Zephyr's back in the same pattern as Sen's without anything to go on except her memories and the mental communication between us.

The moment we were both sitting on his back, Zephyr flew us up into the air, the cavern wide enough he could just about fly tight circles over the heads of everyone inside.

We went around twice, and then Zephyr tucked his wings in and rolled while we were still on him. All three of us were in freefall for a moment, and the mythicals below us screamed and gasped, but the air I controlled responded quickly to my commands.

I blasted all three of us with enough air from below that we slowed and came to a halt a few yards above the crowd. Zephyr was the hardest to hold, but all three of us remained in the air while I moved us back to the circle we'd started in.

Instead of gently lowering all three of us, I reached for the earth and, while keeping the air and us steady, I lifted three pedestals of rock up to meet us as we touched down.

This gained me several cheers, but I didn't stop there. Over the next minute, I lowered the rock again, doing my best to keep it steady as we descended.

Finally, we stood on the cavern floor again, a slight circle around each of us the only sign that I'd changed anything at all. Cheering and clapping erupted from the entire cavern of spectators, and even Sierrathen had a delighted look in her eyes. It wasn't the hardest thing I could do, but it had shown what both of my companions were capable of, and then I had mirrored it using my powers

I grinned as once again, Sierrathen struggled to get silence so she could talk one last time and declare our bonding successful. It seemed no one was listening, however.

Let me help, Zephyr said into my head before he flapped his powerful wings again. He was soon in the air, then he opened his mouth and roared. I used the air to help him project, bouncing it off the walls and back in on everyone to compound the effect as it continued. By the time he finished, the cavern had begun to shake.

Immediately I rushed all the air downwards and dampened it, creating a silencing effect I'd had no idea was possible. I also lifted the circle of rock Sierrathen was on so she stood a couple of feet taller than the crowds.

Sierrathen recovered from her shock quickly enough to seize the opportunity and speak.

"It is clear that the bond is firm. Aella has bonded with both Zephyr and the air element and Sen and the earth element. They have been tested and found to be strong and united. Let us respect the honor bestowed upon them."

This seemed to end the ceremony, the words sounding official and as if they were expected. I had not stuck around through all of Erlan's ceremony so I wasn't sure, but it signaled the end, and many of the elven masters now came forward, smiling and clapping. Even Seth came with them, the elf reaching me first.

"Nicely done," Seth said quietly and made a show of

petting Sen. "I'm willing to confess I'm glad we're on the same side, elf."

"The feeling is mutual," I replied, thinking of what he could do with fire that I couldn't. Being allies worked, even if I still didn't like him much.

For the next few minutes, I could do little but accept people's congratulations and hold Sen close so I could keep an eye on her. She leaned into me as more and more people came to talk to us, clearly overwhelmed by the sheer numbers.

When I thought enough was enough, I started moving toward the exit, the elven masters coming with me, making it clear they had something they wanted to say more than just congratulating me.

The crowds were already dispersing a little, which made it easier to get outside, but I glanced back a couple of times to see the council was all staying behind and having a very animated discussion. I would need to come back and talk to them, but I wanted to start with the elven masters. If there was still a chance I was washing my hands of the place, then I wanted to get what information I could before I did.

It felt a little strange to be thinking in those terms, especially when I'd just told Seth I wanted to be considered an ally, but I needed them to respect me even if they didn't agree with everything I did. And we had to work together against humanity's aggressors. But I'd told Sierrathen I wouldn't stick around if I wasn't respected, and I meant it. She'd have to finish convincing the council. I'd done every-thing I could already.

Finally, it was just me, the four elven masters, and a

couple of others I'd grown to like and trust standing in a clearing to one side of the cavern network.

Orthelo no longer had the phoenix on his shoulder, but I noticed a furry creature draped around his neck, a small foxlike face nestled under his chin. Was this his bonded animal?

"You promised me answers," I said as soon as I had the earth master's attention. "What's so special about me bonding with more than one element? You've all led me to believe it's not possible but encouraged me to try anyway. I showed it was beginning to be possible several months ago when we fought the soldiers last, but only now when I've bonded with Sen do you react this way. Why?"

Ruehnar, the water master, was the first to step forward and look as if he might answer my question.

"A long time ago, when Tuviel was the leader of a great elven race and she took them into battle, they banished a dark elf who had given his soul to the evil of another world in exchange for great power. He could break the bonds of other elves, claiming their creatures for his own. He almost tore the bond from Tuviel and Azargad themselves."

I gasped as I thought of how awful something like that must have felt and reached for Zephyr as he leaned into me and Sen hugged the side of my neck. This was something we clearly didn't want.

"Although Tuviel and Azargad were victorious, the solution was to close the portals between the worlds. We've always known that one day the evil could return. It showed us what was possible, however. A being powerful enough to form more than one bond, and to control more than one element."

"And that's where I come in," I said, exhaling.

I didn't like the sound of where this was going, but I realized it wasn't the first time I'd heard of it. Minsheng had mentioned that the organization had trained Shishous and were looking out for elves with strong bonds for some sort of prophecy. Was this related?

"Let me guess. A group of folks decided they'd try and find someone this powerful so when the evil returned, they would be able to protect everyone."

"Yes. And no," Orthelo replied. "There were several different groups who had different ideas of what should be done. Some went to seek answers. They came back with the prophecy the organization follows, although it cost them dearly. They have been operating for centuries, waiting for the elf to come along, always believing that one of their kind would find the powerful elf born to save us all."

"And the others?" I demanded, knowing I was sounding snippy but not sure I cared, given this was my life everyone was now discussing.

"The Sanctuary formed, hoping to nurture an elf in peace with compassion for all races."

"Well, you failed there," I replied, anger beginning to make me tense. "You excluded humanity and became a frightened—"

Aella, careful, Zephyr's voice growled. *You have every right to be angry, but insults won't do anything but close their minds. Give them the respect you ask for.*

I exhaled and closed my eyes as Zephyr moved even closer, letting me lean my head into him as he projected his calm my way.

"I'm sorry," I said when I felt calmer. "Insults help no one. Not everything about the Sanctuary is bad by a very long way."

"You have a good point and are right about the lack of humans. An us-and-them mentality has formed. On both sides," Ruehnar said, the water elf reaching for me and placing a hand on my shoulder.

"The other groups?" I asked, getting back on point.

"We believe another group of elves or mythicals exists in the shadows somewhere. A group who literally gave birth to you."

"And then abandoned me to the world," I replied, but it made sense. Someone had ensured I had the warehouse and had found Zephyr, and we still had no idea who.

"Then there's those who would open the portals back up and take the fight to the evil. The ones who are just waiting for the right moment to strike. I expect to see some of those become more obvious. And there are rumors some of those would relish the power on the other side having control instead," Aquilan, the air master, said, his bushy eyebrows coming together in a deep frown as he spoke.

The seriousness of his expression made me pay attention. Whoever this group was, they were clearly something he feared.

"There's no evidence to suggest they still exist or that they're any kind of cohesive force," Orthelo replied. "We're worrying Aella unnecessarily to inform her of those."

"We didn't know the sect trying to create the powerful elf existed until Aella walked into the Sanctuary and told us who she was," Ruehnar pointed out.

So be careful, I thought. *There are more groups than we might know.*

Outwardly, I merely sighed. It seemed having multiple bonds had done something impressive, but...

It only happened after you put those bracers on and could feel Sen coming, Zephyr finished for me. I looked to Zephyr as I nodded, knowing the others wouldn't entirely understand what he'd suggested.

Instead of telling them, I showed them, pulling up my jacket sleeves and revealing the bracers I now wore. Orthelo reached forward immediately and touched them, his eyes shining and wet as if he remembered them.

"I put these on only yesterday for the first time. I bonded with Sen only a few hours later."

"They were said to enhance the elemental bond with the earth," Orthelo explained. "But alone they wouldn't have made the bond happen if that is what you fear."

"No, but it might be worth us finding the other artifacts. If Aella is truly descended from them all anyway, they belong to her by rights." Ruehnar bounded, his eyes shining with excitement.

"Which is exactly why I gave her the bracers," Sierrathen said from behind us. I wheeled around to see not only her but the entire Sanctuary council behind her. It looked like we were about to have a little chat.

CHAPTER SIX

"I understand you didn't ask for any of this, Aella," Sierrathen said as she cut across another of the council members again and motioned for the dwarf to calm. "But you are in this position now."

I sighed and leaned into Zephyr again, grateful I was never alone if nothing else. I wasn't some mystical chosen one. I had sentient companions who were just as much a part of this as I was. And if the prophecy was to be believed, there might even be more out there I was supposed to bond with.

After Sierrathen had come to me and the other elven masters I'd followed her to the council chambers and joined the rest of the Sanctuary council. It wasn't the perfect place to be for Zephyr, the roof a little too low, but it was where all the important conversations had to happen.

"It's important you don't harm the humans further," I said. "Will you at least concede this point? They may have trespassed, but we need to follow correct procedures and pursue justice in a way that the American people can accept if we wish to gain any amount of trust."

"If I had my way they'd all be dead now, their lives sacrificed to the orders they felt were so important to obey. It might make those who would attack think twice." Vestan stood back, his fists bunched.

"It would, but it also has you leading out of fear, and I'd rather gain respect in other ways," I shot back, not entirely sure I sounded like myself. Was I really mature enough to see this in the actions of others?

"We'll turn over the humans," Lorcan said, his word no doubt having the final say on the matter. After all, he was in charge of the Sanctuary's security. "If you could assist in having them brought to justice, it would aid us greatly. We want them charged with both trespassing and with violence."

I nodded. Although I wasn't completely sure how I'd go about it, I was pretty sure Minsheng and Chris would be able to help me work it out. It was the best outcome. A peace offering.

"Now, I need to get back to the warehouse as soon as possible," I said as the tiredness of the whole adventure began to rear its ugly head.

It was lunchtime, and I still hadn't slept. Only adrenaline and constant need to be doing and moving had kept me awake so far. The council had had me sitting in their chamber for at least half an hour.

I got to my feet as I forced my eyes to remain open. Lorcan and Sierrathen did the same, but I noticed the others remained seated. They all acknowledged my intent to leave, however. As far as meeting with the Sanctuary council had gone, it wasn't the worst.

As he'd escorted me in, Lorcan walked with me to the Sanctuary borders.

"They will come around in time," he said. "It may not feel like it yet, but I believe you've made progress today in changing their minds about you."

"I know I didn't grow up here, and there are many elven and mythicals traditions I know nothing of, but I am doing my best. We're all doing our best."

"And in truth, they're grateful," Lorcan replied, his voice deep and tinged with sadness.

"They've got a funny way of showing it." I stopped as we reached the border and bowed to the centaur. He was taller than me by a fair amount, but Zephyr was taller again, and I marveled at the variety of creatures we represented.

"Keep them safe," I said as I reached for the air around me and prepared to fly. I let Sen know to tuck herself up safe in my jacket again.

"As always. Do the same for those with you, and pass any messages you need to via Ronan. I'm sure we can find a path through this difficult time, even if it requires us to embrace a path less trodden or one we would not normally choose for ourselves."

"I'm starting to think it's always the path less trodden or that's least appealing," I replied with a wry smile before I pushed up and into the air.

Zephyr flew up behind me and I found myself growing more and more relaxed as I climbed, putting all my cares and worries behind me again for a while.

We headed back west and toward LA, coming together in the air so I could ride on Zephyr's back once more.

You okay? I asked Zephyr only a few minutes into our flight.

Yes. I think. This trip has given us much to think about but also given us more strength. I also won't deny I feel grateful for Sierrathen's actions and getting to perform the bonding ceremony properly. It might be something small to most, but...

It makes you feel valued.

Exactly.

I sighed and sent waves of love in Zephyr's direction, showing him how I felt about him instead of saying it. I might be equally bonded with Sen and Zephyr, but there was still something deeper and different about my relationship with the dragon. Something that more time bonded to Sen wouldn't necessarily create.

This time we were flying in daylight so we moved even higher in the sky and tried not to attract too much attention to ourselves. It wasn't easy keeping our speed up, however.

The lack of sleep was taking its toll on all of us, our concentration slipping sometimes.

We were about three-quarters of the way when I yawned one too many times. I couldn't keep going like this. I was feeling my control of the air slip, and it was making it harder for us to fly safely. On top of that, Sen had curled herself up a little lower in my jacket and gone to sleep herself, her mind projecting warm, dreamlike thoughts.

Can you fly lower and look for a store? I asked Zephyr. *I need to get some caffeine or something.*

I'd love a decent snack too. Lunch was great, but it wasn't chips and soda.

I shook my head at the way Zephyr liked junk food now. It had occurred to me that it was possibly slightly irresponsible of me to get my bonded mythical hooked on junk food, but I could barely talk. At least we were often active.

Zephyr swooped lower while I held on tightly, reducing my control to just the barrier I held around myself. I'd extended it a little to protect Sen as well, but for now, I didn't want to have lots to focus on. It meant Zephyr was flying without my help, but he appeared to be the best one of us at coping without sleep. He was made for flying and being active for long periods.

It didn't take long to spot a store and Zephyr flew even lower, circling the building on the edge of a town a couple of times before we landed in the parking lot. It was fairly busy so we had to be careful. Even then, a few people squealed.

"It's okay, we're friendly," I yelled as we moved lower and touched down. Sen jolted awake. I felt a little bad about disturbing her, but she quickly realized we were landing and scurried back to the top of my zipper so she could peek out at the human world.

I felt her shock at the strange cars moving around and grinned. It seemed she'd not encountered them before.

Her delight and curiosity took my mind off the awkward looks I was getting and the people warily hurrying past.

The store we'd landed at had the large double automatic doors at the entrance so I motioned for Zephyr to come too. The sooner everyone got used to a dragon popping into their shop, the better. Maybe we could do some good PR while we were here.

Remember to smile, Zephyr said into my head a moment later, sounding cheerfully amused as he did. I chuckled and waved at a young boy sitting on a trike, his mouth open.

"Want to come pet Zephyr?" I asked, getting my own back in one sentence. The kid's mom immediately shook her head and tried to steer the trike away from the store, however.

I sighed but I kept my smile in place and looked for others to be pleasant too. Few were willing to meet my gaze, but I saw some older teenagers just inside the first set of doors, and I waved at them.

"Come say hi to him," I said, Zephyr stopping by the doors and lowering his head a little. He tucked his wings tight to his sides and waddled toward the opening.

One of the girls in the group let out a slight squeal as he moved even closer, his head only a couple of feet from the boldest-looking male.

"Hello," Zephyr said a moment later. The teenager's eyes went wide, but he stayed where he was.

"Hi," he stammered out.

"Oh, you have my favorite chips. Aella says I shouldn't eat too many of them, but they're so delicious."

This made the girl chuckle, and the guy took the chips from the top of the shopping bag and held them out.

"Do...do you want them?" he asked.

"Nah, you're good. I'll buy him some of his own. I think he's just trying to make conversation. He doesn't get to talk to as many people as he likes," I said before I moved past him and looked for the aisle where I could grab a few snacks and drinks without needing to go deeper into the shop.

The teenagers visibly relaxed at this, and the kid shoved his bag of chips back in his shopping bag, also relieved.

"Have you tried the extra-cheesy ones?" the kid asked. "I think they're even better, but they don't sell them here."

"I haven't. I'll ask Aella to get them for me next time."

"Can you not get them yourself?" one of the girls asked as I started moving away.

"I'm not usually allowed inside the store. I think I'm a bit big for some of the aisles now, and I'm not very good at steering the shopping carts. I always get the ones with dodgy wheels," I heard him say over my shoulder. The teenagers laughed and moved closer. Leaving him to it, I hurried over to the energy drinks and grabbed a couple.

Then, to make it up to my best friend and show him I was listening, I grabbed a handful of bags of the same chips and made for the ten items and under checkout.

I could get through the self-serve lanes, so I did, but there was a store worker keeping an eye on them, and she was clearly doing her job because she exclaimed as soon as I stopped in front of one.

"Oh, my, what is that creature in your jacket? It's so cute!"

"This is Sen," I replied, turning slightly so she could get a better look. "Sen is a wood sprite or dryad. A bit like a sentient mushroom."

"A sentient mushroom?" someone else asked on the checkout in between us, looking over as he did.

"Yeah, a mythical. This is her first time in a store."

Sen waved a moment later and gave them both a large smile. The store worker let out a delighted squeak and waved back, but the other shopper didn't seem to know what to do.

I finished my transaction and we both waved again before I picked everything up and made my way back to the front of the store. I got back to find several members of store security standing in the atrium trying to encourage Zephyr to back up a bit despite him only having his head through the doorway.

The teenagers were still with him, and their body language very clearly put them between the security men and Zephyr.

"It's okay; he's with me," I said as I came closer. *You okay?* I asked Zephyr.

I am, now that you got my favorite chips.

Unable to help it, I laughed and gained a glare or two from the security as they turned to me.

"You need to get your dragon away from the store. We don't allow pets in here."

"He's not a pet," I replied without missing a beat. "I'm assuming you tried to tell them that, Zephyr?" I asked.

"But you said he was with you," the nearest security guard shot back.

"Yeah, with me, not owned by me."

"No one owns me," Zephyr said, loudly enough everyone could hear. "I'm not a slave."

There was silence as more and more people realized the dragon could talk.

I deliberately moved to his side, the teenagers parting to let me through. Opening a bag of the chips along the way, I ignored the stares. When he opened his mouth, I dumped the whole bag inside, and he closed his eyes and let out a deep rumble of approval.

The teenagers laughed, and I held out the rest of the chip bags.

"Anyone else want to help him with these while I chug my drink?" I asked.

There wasn't a shortage of volunteers, and the chips were being fed one by one to Zephyr.

The security backed up a little, although I glanced their way and saw them talking on radios. It wasn't over, but for now, we had a reprieve I intended to utilize.

While Zephyr continued to make friends and people grew braver around him, I focused on letting Sen try a few different chips while I drank the energy drink to wake myself up.

The excited myconid also drew some attention and nibbled on each chip with little squeals of delight of her own. Pretty soon I had cheese dust all over the opening of my jacket and all over her, much to the amusement of our audience.

Before I could get back to Zephyr's side and suggest we get back in the air, there were shouts from outside the shop and somewhere behind Zephyr.

"Back up from the store and don't make any sudden movements," a commanding male voice bellowed from the parking lot.

A quick glance at the security guards showed me three smug faces. Wasting no time, I pushed out of the store and hurried around Zephyr to see who was trying to get him to move.

I came face to face with a couple of large army vehicles and at least twenty soldiers. Many of them carried guns, and they were aimed at Zephyr.

"I said back up from the store," the man commanded again.

"He's with me," I repeated, reaching out for him and running my hand down his side, his smooth scales warm under the light of the early afternoon sun.

You might want to slowly back up, I added.

Slowly Zephyr started to turn while I watched the soldiers. A couple of them gulped as they found themselves now facing a large dragon, and a few of them adjusted their grips on their guns. They were nervous.

"Is there a problem?" I asked. "We were just getting snacks and having a chat."

"You're not welcome here," the commanding officer said, not even looking at me.

I moved to stand right in front of Zephyr, throwing up an air wall no one but us would know was there just in case.

"Why not? I'm an American citizen and a normal customer. No one refused me service, and we paid with dollars just like anyone else. There's no threat here."

The commander finally looked at me.

"Are you who I think you are?" he demanded.

"If you mean, am I Aella, then yes. I'm her, but as I said, we just stopped for snacks and drinks. Perhaps it's best if we get back in the air and back to LA. We're clearly much more welcome in the stores there."

"We can't let you do that," the commander said. "You

need to come with us. You might be trying to do all sorts. I can't just let you walk away."

"Are you trying to arrest me?" I demanded, starting to feel myself tense. This wasn't good. I didn't want to be taken but I didn't want to start a fight either.

"Come on, guys, stand down or something. We were eating chips together. No big deal. No threat. No crime." The first teenage guy appeared at my side, both his hands up in the universal sign of peace.

"We can't accept that. We have to take the dragon in. It's a vicious animal and—"

"No, I'm not," Zephyr interrupted, his voice full of indignance.

I could have laughed at the shock on all their faces. Did none of these people watch the news? Zephyr had talked on-air two or three times now, and everyone still assumed he was a mindless beast.

"I'll have you know I have an IQ of one hundred and sixty-seven. I'm brighter than Einstein was, and I'm a good deal more good-looking on top." Zephyr lifted his head and shook out his wings.

I fought to keep a serious expression.

Really? One-six-seven? I asked him.

Erlan had me do one of those internet tests. Said there was no way I could beat his score.

You know those things give you higher scores than the official tests, right?

Zephyr sighed, but the commander continued to move forward.

"You're coming with us. If you don't cooperate, we will use force." The officer sounded even more angry and determined and I took a deep breath. This didn't bode well. This guy wasn't going to back down.

"We're not doing anything because we don't have to," I replied. "Firstly, you've given us no reason to be arrested. And secondly, if you've watched any of the videos out there, you'll have noticed I was fighting the agency charged with hunting mythicals down and you'll know that you don't have anywhere near enough firepower or men to force us to do anything we don't want to do. So I'll ask nicely one last time before we decide to head on our way. What are you trying to arrest us for? And don't give me any bullshit."

I would have folded my arms across my chest had Sen not been in the way, so I had to settle for glaring.

"I don't have to explain myself to you, civilian," he snapped back. "Get out of the way," he said to the kid.

I shook my head, but I then turned to the teenager still beside me.

"You should go back inside. This is likely to get ugly and I wouldn't want you to get hurt. The bullets bounce off Zephyr."

The teenager looked between the soldiers and me.

"We'll be fine, don't worry. They could empty every single one of those guns at us and do no more than make noise, but I don't want anyone else getting hurt."

This was enough to convince the kid, and he hurried away.

"I won't ask again," the commander said as soon as we were clear of others.

"And I won't warn you again. Don't start a fight you can't win for no good reason."

The commander didn't respond but yelled for the men to start firing. I pushed on the air wall as hard as I could, but Zephyr swept his leg around me and blocked my skin anyway.

Get into the air, he yelled into my head.

What about you?

I can't risk them shooting my wings, he replied. *Get in the air and then deal with their guns. I'll make sure no one else gets hurt.*

I put one hand to my chest to hold Sen safe and then blasted my body out from Zephyr's side and into the air. None of the soldiers followed me, but the air wall felt like it was being ripped to pieces by the sheer number of bullets firing through it. One or two got through and hit the scales on Zephyr's chest.

Growling and more than a little pissed, I used my abilities to hurl concentrated blasts of air at the weapons, forcing them all downward so they hit the ground instead.

Shards flew into the air, going in all directions, some hitting the soldiers. None of them dropped their weapons, however. It was as if the guns were glued to their hands.

Not sure what else to do, I suggested Zephyr exhale, but he was already ahead of me and shifting his body to access the paralyzing vapor.

It poured out of him and I took control of it, making sure it swept over all the soldiers. Some of them tried to flee, but I had the white cloud moving fast enough to catch them.

Silence fell as I slowly landed beside Zephyr again and whipped the remaining gas up into the air so no innocent bystanders were caught up in it. It swirled and dissipated above, revealing the soldiers all fixed in strange positions where they'd fallen.

"Wow," I heard a familiar voice declare from behind me.

I turned to see the group of teenagers coming out of the shop first. Two of them had their cell phones in their hands, no doubt videoing me again.

"Will they be okay?" the guy recording asked.

"Yes. It just paralyzes them for a while. It will wear off. They might have a few bruises from falling over, but nothing else."

"And you did all that while they were trying to shoot you?"

"I really don't want to hurt anyone," I said. "And where I have the choice, I won't. But if people keep treating us like a threat and shooting at us for no reason, we might hurt them accidentally while defending ourselves. Other mythicals are also likely to run out of patience. We just want to live, to go to the shops. To eat chips, make friends and fly."

With my final words, I nodded at Zephyr, and he spread his wings. It was time to get out of here before we attracted any more trouble.

CHAPTER SEVEN

The rest of our journey proved uneventful, thankfully, but as soon as we got close to our warehouse in the middle of LA, I saw Daisy waiting for us on the roof.

She waved as a smile spread across her face, and immediately I felt myself relax. It was good to be home.

Zephyr circled to get the best approach and brought us in to land, touching down with perfection before folding his wings.

I used my powers to jet myself up and off his back, the motion quicker. No sooner had I landed than Daisy came to give me a hug, but I had to put up a hand and stop her from crushing Sen.

"Wow, I've heard of little sprites in mushroom form but they're so much cuter than I imagined," she declared.

I introduced them, letting Sen squeak out her own name a couple of times, but said no more. I didn't want to have to repeat myself, and I had more than one tale to tell.

"Where is everyone?" I asked. "Is Minsheng here?"

"Yes, and we saw the news report on your little run-in at the store. Come on, I'm sure you've got lots to tell us."

I nodded, grateful Daisy knew me well enough to usher me inside. We made our way all the way to the bottom floor and the table in the kitchen, the place we had all our important talks.

Along the way I pointed a few things out to Sen, feeling guilty that I wasn't giving her a full tour of the building. It couldn't be helped, however. There were bigger things to discuss. I'd just had soldiers try and take Zephyr and me in.

I found Minsheng where we expected, but he knew enough to give me a hug before anything else, meaning I had to defend Sen a second time.

"First things first," I said. "What's the reaction to what happened?"

"Actually fairly positive overall," Daisy replied. "Although it just brings attention to us again when ideally quiet might be better if we want the protesters to go away."

I nodded. We'd already agreed that not being in the limelight too much might help. Having the press and society in general move on to whatever the next big event was might make them chill out a little regarding us, but I'd just set that plan back a fair amount between the recent incidents at the beach and now coming back from the Sanctuary. It wasn't ideal. I looked anything but peaceful now.

Trying not to panic, I listened as Minsheng, Daisy, Chris, and Ronan all talked over how I'd handled it. Everyone agreed I'd done a fairly good job in a difficult situation.

"I think it's best you only travel at night when no one can see you," Minsheng said at the end.

"Yeah, I think you're probably right."

"And maybe we can find a way to block people recording you for now," Chris said, turning as if to go and begin doing something about it.

"No," I replied. "That only makes it look like we've got something to hide. We're going to have to let them video us."

Chris frowned but didn't argue, sitting back down again.

With the pause in conversation, I decided to make the most of it and lifted Sen up in the palm of my hand.

"The most interesting part of this whole trip was this wonderful creature, however," I continued. "Sen and I bonded on the way to the Sanctuary."

"Bonded, as in, just like you and Zephyr?" Daisy asked, her mouth falling open. Minsheng's eyebrows lifted, and he leaned in closer to get a good look at the myconid.

I grinned and told them everything that had happened and I'd learned at the Sanctuary, including the uneasy truce and the progress I'd made in a few quarters regarding my popularity. I'd had a frostier reception to the great city when I'd first found it, but being the person to tell the world that mythicals existed had made their attitude toward me far worse.

Not all mythicals had wanted the human race to know they weren't alone, and even fewer had thought I should be the one to get to choose when and how to blow the whistle. And maybe they were right, but I'd done what I thought was right at the time, and I couldn't undo it now.

Everyone continued to admire Sen while I tried to describe how bonding with her had felt. Finally, I revealed my last secret. The bracers I was now wearing.

"Oh, were they in that package?" Daisy asked. "I thought it felt strange when we were moving your room and I found it. I meant to ask you, but...there's always so much going on."

It was an admission that put my mind at ease, but we needed to decide how to progress. I needed to do something about this mess and I was also eager to see what I was capable of now that I was bonded with Sen and wearing the bracers, but a yawn interrupted my train of thought and I knew sleep was going to need to come first.

After briefly showing Sen some of the rest of the building, all three of us settled into the large bedroom put aside for us. I could hear workmen now and then, but they weren't drilling or hammering so it could have been worse.

When Sen saw my flowerpot and the tree sapling inside it, she ran down my body and over to it before climbing the unit of shelves it stood on, using her root-like feet to flick herself upward in a strange jump before latching on with her hands. She then settled down on the soil at its base and closed her eyes.

Guess that's as good a place as any for her to sleep, Zephyr said into my head. *I'm sticking to the bed though, if that's all right with everyone.*

No complaints from me as long as you promise not to snore.

My conscience wouldn't let me commit to such a thing. Alas, it is too difficult.

I chuckled before the two of us curled up together, his tail wrapped around both of us. As I drifted off, I thought of how worried I'd been about him at the store and every-thing else that had happened. Although Zephyr had been worried that Sen bonding with me would be detrimental to our existing bond, I felt as if it had actually strengthened it.

Before now, I'd worried that the only reason I felt anything for the dragon was because of the magic in our bond. But my bond with Sen was different. It already felt like the bond between friends. Good friends who could always relax together and pick up where they left off after any length of break.

My doubt that I loved Zephyr was gone. He had my heart.

"Let's do some training," Minsheng said as Zephyr and I finished our late dinner, seeming like he'd read my mind. Sen had spent the entire meal with her roots in a glass of water with a tiny bit of plant food added, courtesy of Daisy and the organization finding information on the myconid variety of dryads while we slept.

Almost everyone living in the warehouse was still up, and many had eaten with me despite the late hour. I'd noticed over the last few weeks that almost everyone's hours were shifting later and later. Going out at night was safer and it was also when the protesters mostly went home. Only a couple were die-hards and angry enough to camp out.

"I'd like to try a few archery-related skills with you as well," Ronan said, bowing as he did. "I believe those bracers will increase your skill with the weapon, and while it's not perfect for these times, perhaps the advantage will make enough of a difference."

"Hmmm..." Chris said before anyone could move. "I might have an idea. Let me know if the bracers do make the archery better."

I lifted my eyebrows, but Chris walked off without any more of an explanation, and I was ushered toward the dojo part of the warehouse. It was time to train.

The room was empty except for us, the night too late for the dojo to still be operating, but Lyra was still there, the room tidy, but the woman sitting at a small table in one corner quickly going over the financial books for her business.

She looked up when she saw me and squealed in delight when Sen scurried across the floor, the small creature enjoying the space and appearing to have a lot more energy after the big drink.

"That has to be the cutest mythical I've ever seen," Lyra declared.

I gave her a moment to admire the small creature and let Zephyr also get started on his exercises. At least the ones he was capable of while indoors.

I decided to start with archery. It would help me determine if my new bond helped my aim and also whether being rested when using it would make a difference. I'd not needed to use my abilities at all since I'd woken up.

Ronan quickly fetched two bows and a quiver of target practice arrows from one of the equipment cupboards. Grinning, I took the ones I didn't recognize as well, knowing the other was his from his days at the Sanctuary.

We got into position in front of the archery targets, several in a line against one wall. Ronan had been running an archery range and lessons here for several months now, and it was yet another needed income stream for the building.

"Why don't we do a set of ten arrows and see how well you do without any extra magic or aids. Just shoot and see what happens," Ronan suggested.

Like a baseline, I thought, knowing I wasn't the most amazing at shooting a bow yet. After all this time trying to use a gun and training with one, I wasn't used to the different method with the bow. Shooting higher than the target because the projectile curved in the air felt strange.

Despite that, I took a deep breath and slowly let it back out again, shooting at the end of the exhale before I could draw in another lungful of air and before my body could demand it and distract me. The arrow flew, Ronan firing not long later. As it often did, my arrow hit the target but not very near the center.

I still had a lot of practicing to do.

The rest of the arrows came quickly, my mind getting back into a pattern I'd practiced before. It was hard not to use my air magic too much, my body so often connected to the air around me it was almost automatic to move and manipulate it. It helped the arrows fly in a straighter line and not curve so much when I fired, but it wasn't ideal either. Most of the time, I used normal weapons to give my magic a break. Using it to make the arrows more accurate didn't give me a break.

"You're improving," Ronan said once our arrows were spent and he was checking my score sheet. "This was your best non-magic score. Why don't we try it with magic now? Just your air."

I nodded and took the arrows back. I'd not thought of testing my two affinities separately but we would need to in order to truly see if I'd gained something from my earth connection and the bracers I wore.

This second set of arrows hit nearer the center, my mind making a cleaner, easier funnel of air for the arrow to go down. At the speed it was traveling and over such a short distance, it didn't have much of an impact, but it was enough.

About ten minutes later, Ronan held up another score-card that was clearly higher, and a quick calculation in my head pegged it at just over ten points more. Although we'd practiced several times in the past, this was the first time we'd performed some kind of direct comparison.

It made me grateful for my abilities but aware of how much better I could be at the task. With practice and my abilities on top, I might be able to get very accurate. Especially as I hadn't attempted to combine both my elements yet.

As I fetched the arrows back and we got back in place to try a third set of shots, I concentrated on reaching for the plant component of the arrow I held. Although it was made of wood and the same thing as the plants I usually controlled, it felt different immediately. More resistant to my attempts to connect.

I was sure I wouldn't have been able to connect at all before I'd put on the bracers. They were boosting what I could feel and control. The arrow was like something dead but still yielding to basic instructions. A tool, but not alive.

It made me wonder if the tree was aware of its death when we chopped it down or lopped off its branches. Something was clearly taken away when it died. Something I could now feel.

Ronan was beside me and preparing to fire before I could process all these new thoughts.

"Ready?" he asked as he looked my way.

"Almost," I replied as I finished focusing and tried to move the arrow.

It rolled over in my hand and I almost dropped it, but that was all the confirmation I needed that I could establish a connection. It was time to give two-strand magic archery a try.

Once again, I made air tunnels and used that to help, but I also tried to guide the arrow with my mind after I'd fired it. At first I seemed to make it worse, the first two shots going wide, but the third hit the center color, and the next did as well.

By the time I'd done all ten, over half of them were good-score arrows. The kind that professional archers would have been proud of. We looked over my score card and I broke into a broad grin. If the first two shots hadn't gone so far out, it would have been my best score ever. As it was, it tied.

"It seems you're going to be a decent archer after all," Ronan declared, a strange light I couldn't interpret in his eyes.

"Let's try guns next and see what you can do with those too," Daisy said from a few yards away, having come to watch at some point.

Ronan bowed at me and then Daisy as well before

going to his room for his weekly meeting with Lorcan. Centaurs could communicate telepathically when they were far away and with others by way of a strange stone.

I'd been offered one once before, and it linked Ronan and I, something rare. The stones were almost never used outside of safe havens.

Ronan and Lorcan were counterparts, Lorcan responsible for the security of the Sanctuary and Ronan responsible for the security of the dojo, at least for now. Ronan had been one of the senior border guards at the Sanctuary before he'd chosen to come with me and try to change the world.

Normally there was plenty for the two centaurs to discuss, but I knew they'd want to check in with each other even if I'd already passed on most of the information already.

As Daisy became my sole companion besides Sen and Zephyr in the dojo area of the building, I settled into my usual routine for a while. There was always plenty of training to do, and it kept me focused. I wasn't done fighting yet, and who knew what trick I practiced might save my life?

CHAPTER EIGHT

As Sen flew around the sky over the warehouse on Zephyr's back, I felt strangely bereft. It was a test. We were trying to work out if the bond between Sen and me was as strong as the bond between Zephyr and I, and we were also trying to work on some battle strategies.

I watched them get higher and higher, the feeling in my stomach of some kind of thread unraveling and tugging on my insides as it did that accompanied Zephyr and now Sen getting farther away already present.

Everything okay up there? I asked.

For now, Zephyr replied.

Sen high. Sen cold.

I frowned. *Do you want to come back down?*

Sen continue, the myconid added.

Although I considered making her come back down, I let them keep flying, my link and the feel of them in my head getting more distant. It didn't feel great, but equally, it had felt worse before.

Over time my bond had grown stronger, and the

distance we'd been able to go and still be connected had increased. This was the first time we'd actually tested it, however.

It was part of our conditions with the organization. If we gave them information and helped them understand the bonds between mythicals and what elementals were capable of, Erlan and I got paid. It was something Minsheng and Chris had both fought for as the new costs of the warehouse and the extra floor became apparent.

The organization was also paying for the build, something thankfully now almost complete, but they weren't paying any of the bills, and the protesters always outside the dojo had cut Lyra's numbers in her training sessions. That also meant less rent.

So here I was, testing something the organization wanted to know less than half an hour before a news crew was due to turn up to do an exclusive interview in my home. We weren't showing them around the whole thing, but enough of it that Daisy and the others had made it spotless.

Yet another reason I was out here. I didn't want to be dusting when I didn't even want to do the interview. It was necessary, however. Public opinion on us wasn't awful, but Jacobs had been on TV again recently, and people we suspected were on his payroll had analyzed the recent incidents in every possible way.

Despite our attempts to be nice and not hurt anyone, we'd been painted as the bad guy. People wanted to know why we didn't simply hand ourselves over and let the courts of justice declare us innocent if we were. It wasn't quite that simple. There wasn't an active investigation against us. Not even against the men the Sanctuary had captured and then released to us.

Chris had taken them to the cops and, thanks to him looking more human than some of the rest of us and having a normal job, they'd listened as he'd explained what had happened and how we wanted to press charges for trespassing and violent assault.

Of course, it was a little more complicated than that, but Chris had promised it was going in a good direction. There was even a lawyer helping him out.

As the gap increased, I checked in with Zephyr and Sen again. Zephyr was about as small as my finger in the sky above now and still climbing and getting farther away.

I can still hear you, but you're starting to feel...less there, Zephyr replied.

There was nothing from Sen.

Is Sen okay? I asked, fear making me reach for the air around me and prepare to fly up, my eyes fixed on my dragon.

Yes, I can still talk to her. I found a warmer current of air up here so she's not quite so cold.

I exhaled and reminded myself to relax.

The reporting team will be here soon. I think I should come back down, and we should put my current altitude as the maximum distance for now. I don't want to push it any further. It feels really uncomfortable.

Ditto. Come back down. I'm going to see if we can work out when Sen and I reconnect.

Zephyr didn't reply, but I saw him change shape and tilt his head downwards a little. Of course, he had to be careful with Sen. we'd tried to make her a small bag to sit in, but that didn't mean she was completely safe and Zephyr could do whatever he wanted.

I watched them come lower and called for Sen periodically. It took a minute or two more of Zephyr flying tight circles and coming lower over the building before I felt my connection to the dryad come back, her presence aware to me again.

Sen dropping, she said a moment later, no panic in her voice.

Are you safe in your bag still? I thought, pretty sure she was just saying she was coming back down but wanting to be sure she wasn't saying that she'd fallen out and was dropping back to earth, or anything as scary as that.

Sen safe. Zeph dropping, she clarified. It was the first time she'd attempted his name, and although she had mostly managed it, it still took me by surprise, and I had to think about what she'd said a moment.

I made a note of Zephyr's top altitude and then he shifted even more, trying to drop fairly fast without unseating Sen.

As they got close enough that I could just about see the bag the myconid was sitting in, I used my air ability to still and solidify its position. It meant Zephyr could dive in deeper, knowing Sen was safe and wouldn't fall off his back.

They'd just landed when I heard a voice calling up the stairs and through the building site. It was a Sunday so the builders were taking the day off, but it still took me a moment to pick through the wreckage of tools and half-built rooms to get to the stairs.

Immediately I spotted Emily, another half-elf that I'd

rescued from some of Jacobs' agents and soldiers. She had been living with us ever since, along with her mother, and it made me grin to see her. She'd restyled her hair and was growing it back after Jacobs' agents had cut it all off. It was now a short pixie-like bob.

"The news crew are here and already eager to get set up and record you and the others," Emily informed me as I made my way down the stairs. Sighing, I nodded. It was time to try and persuade the nation to like me. Yet again.

I'd expected a large crew arriving and assistants and all sorts of people for other jobs I didn't understand, but it turned out to be far fewer people than that. Just three stepped out of the van.

One carried the camera and a mic on a stick that he held out over and above the main woman. She was Erika, one of the few women in news reporting right now that I had any respect for. And as far as I was aware, she liked me. She'd also done some homework. Her earliest question when we'd begun communication had been about possibly giving Zephyr his own mic, essentially allowing him to interrupt us if he felt it necessary.

"Aella," she said as she saw me and grinned.

"Hi, Erika," I replied. "Welcome to the warehouse. You've met Zephyr."

I paused as the woman shook my hand and then came closer, clearly considering offering him her hand as she had done me. Zephyr merely dipped his head, almost exactly the way Ronan often did.

"And this is Sen," I added as soon as that part was done. "We've also recently bonded. She's a dryad or a sprite. In particular, a wood sprite or myconid, depending on your folk history."

"You've bonded to another creature? Is that common?"

"Nope. I'm unique as far as we're aware," I replied. "We have no exact idea why, but possibly because I'm descended from one elf of each of the four types."

"Oh wow, so a *Fifth Element* kind of deal. You're literally the fifth element from that Bruce Willis movie," she exclaimed. It prompted me to glance at the camera to see if it was rolling, but the guy holding it was fiddling with something, and I couldn't see any way of working out if it was on or not with just a quick look.

"Well, I don't mind saving the world if I can do it just by kissing a guy, but can I wear my own clothes?" I replied, prompting her and Daisy both to laugh. As my friend made her presence in the background known, Erika motioned for the camera to go that way and moved over as well.

"You must be Daisy, right?" Erika asked. The part-dwarf nodded, one of the few of us who looked human and didn't appear to be able to wield magic at all.

It might have been a sore spot for her in the past, but if it was now, Daisy didn't let it show. Instead, she was there for all of us and was our best marksman. She was also phenomenal as a mythical creature vet.

Erika interviewed Daisy about her role in the battles we had fought and what she thought of what was happening in response to it all.

"As you can see, I'm actually pretty much human," Daisy replied. "And I've lived in LA for many years. All of this mistrust is pointless. All that's changed is that we no longer have to pretend we're something we're not and deny the heritage we have. It's no different to most US folks having Irish blood or Spanish or whatever. We're all American citizens one way or another."

Erika politely brought the conversation to a close and came back to Zephyr, Sen, and me.

"Now, if it's fine with you, I'd like to do a bit of a tour of the place while we ask you a few more questions. Can Zephyr and Sen come with us?"

"For the most part," I replied. There were a few places Zephyr couldn't get into anymore, but nothing that couldn't be avoided. I took Erika up to the main changing area for the dojo, which served as the communal living area the rest of the time.

It was still early for the dojo classes so there was only Erlan there, the elf playing a game on his laptop, Newton sitting on the table beside his arm and pulling strange faces at the antics on the screen.

He paused his game as we came in but didn't get to his feet.

"This is a friend of mine," I replied. "He helps me with the tech side of things and is also a fire elf, bonded with a small fire salamander that we rescued before the agents could capture it last year."

"Is it safe?" Erika asked as we got closer to Newton.

"As long as you don't threaten or overly frighten him," I replied. "He likes to have a scratch just under the chin."

On camera, Erika reached out and slowly scratched Newton's chin while Erlan watched. The fire salamander slowly closed his eyes and clearly leaned into the stimulation.

A moment later, his back lit up with a deep purple flame, making Erika jump. She stopped stroking him.

"Is he supposed to do that?" she asked.

"He does it whenever he feels a strong emotion," I replied. "In this case, pleasure. He really likes having his chin scratched."

"Does he ever get angry?"

"All creatures do," I replied. "But the bond between a creature and their elf is strong and conveys some of the emotions between them. Erlan influences Newton, and sometimes it goes the other way around too."

This returned the woman's attention back to the elf sitting at the table. Again, she asked him a few questions about the battles he'd been in, and we all talked about how we'd demolished the first agency headquarters and how Erlan had helped me make a small tornado and let it loose.

"We're looking into ways we might be able to actually stop them now," I added, interjecting into a slightly different conversation about the twisters. "I want to try to see if I can save lives and homes when we get some of the larger hurricanes making landfall next season."

"For real? You think you've got the power to stop a hurricane?"

"I'm not entirely sure. I know I'm powerful and getting stronger with every day I practice. It's just a matter of time before I'm strong enough. The hard part will be working out when I'm ready to try the first time. I might already be, but we don't know because as far as we're aware, no one alive has ever attempted it before."

Although I'd expected Erika to have a lot more questions on this subject, she seemed to brush it off and keep walking around. I showed her the dojo, introduced her to Ronan, the centaur, and we talked a little of how he was teaching archery and was open to new students. It was helpful to plug it for his sake, and I made sure to include his little school again when Erika finally took an interest in the dojo itself.

Lyra showed up partway through the interview and I shifted the focus to her as well, not exactly comfortable with the question Erika had asked moments before. Apparently, plenty of people wanted to know if I was interested in not being single and who I might fancy as my partner from all around the world.

Answering that I was in love with the dragon I was bonded to struck me as something I wouldn't easily be able to say. It would take a lot of explaining, and even then, I was not sure everyone would understand what was so special about our bond. It would be better if I didn't bring that one up right now.

Thankfully Lyra was only too happy to show the woman around the dojo, and Erika appeared to have forgotten she'd even asked the question when I had her attention back again.

As the woman and film crew left, I sighed with relief and went to tell everyone that it was over for now. The few who wanted to be interviewed as well had done admirable jobs, but I still felt a little annoyed that Crawley hadn't been among them. The ex-agent seemed to be very keen to keep hidden for the whole thing.

I couldn't blame her. Not everyone would understand why she'd reached her position and what she'd done to aid me and why, especially as she'd made it clear she wouldn't mention her daughter at all even if she did talk. Emily was staying out of the limelight.

With everyone relaxing or teaching lessons, I leaned into Zephyr and considered our afternoon.

Want to go to the beach? I asked Zephyr and Sen.

Sen, beach? she asked as Zephyr started walking to the stairs to the top floor. She bounced on three root-like feet and looked up at me.

Of course.

CHAPTER NINE

Although we normally went to the beach at night or late evening, it was afternoon on a gray day as Zephyr flew us closer. Sen was tucked into my jacket, and she cried out in delight as she saw the ocean. I wanted to ask if it was her first time seeing it but it was as if I already knew, her little body wriggling against my torso as she moved to get closer to the view.

I grinned as Zephyr found a quieter spot and swooped down low. People didn't scream when they saw us this time, but only a few waved.

Despite what felt like a colder reception, I waved back anyway. It had been a while since we'd been there in the day, nighttime becoming more and more welcoming. At night we could have a stretch of the sand to ourselves.

Zephyr landed just in the water beyond the safe swimming zone—fewer people there—and splashed the water up. I blasted it away from me to keep from getting wet while I had Sen tucked in my jacket, but again the myconid squealed happily.

Having someone with me who had a fresh excitement for what she was seeing made me feel happier about my decision to come. I wanted to unwind, and here I was away from everyone.

I stayed on Zephyr's back as he strolled along in the shallows, heading south, and Sen climbed out of her little pouch at the front of my jacket up and onto my shoulder, clutching a lock of hair like a safety net and wrapping her root-like feet over my shoulder.

People were looking at us, and some hurried away from the water's edge as we approached, but I continued to smile and wave, thanking anyone who gave us space.

As another group of people approached, Zephyr slowed and walked a little closer to the beach, giving me firmer sand just out of the water to slide off his side onto. This group was a little more elderly, the youngest of them white-haired and walking a dog.

The party of observers stopped about fifty yards away, observing us far more blatantly than younger folks tended to be comfortable doing.

"Hi," I said, walking a little closer, noticing their dog was rather subdued, eyes fixed on Zephyr. Was the animal scared?

The elderly folks didn't reply at first, still looking at the dragon, until one of the closest women leaned toward a gray-haired man beside her, a cane in one of his hands and his other stuffed deep in a pocket.

"Is that the creature on the news?" she asked, no attempt at speaking quietly.

"The dragon thing," he replied. "I believe so."

I moved closer again.

"Hi," I repeated. "I'm Aella. Would you like to meet Zephyr?"

This seemed to get their attention. *I guess they're all a little deaf,* I thought.

Best make sure we speak clearly then. Wouldn't want them thinking we're saying different things," Zephyr replied. *It's bad enough getting some of these humans to understand what we're saying.*

"Meet him?" one of them asked. "I suppose Roger could give him a sniff."

I lifted my eyebrows as the woman with the dog shuffled closer, her dog not seeming to want to come with her at first.

We've got to make friends with the dog before the others will be brave enough? Zephyr asked, his voice sounding delighted at the idea.

Sen like dog, the myconid replied. *Good ride.*

I grinned as I imagined my dryad riding on the back of some wolf-like species of dog in the past.

Yes, she said a moment later, only making me smile all the more. *Ride.*

Not sure we should ride this one without permission, I replied.

Sen crossed her little arms over her chest but stayed on my shoulder.

Although the woman continued to try and persuade Roger to get closer, the dog didn't appear to want to bring itself any nearer to the dragon. I didn't blame it. I wouldn't have wanted to get near a strange animal that could eat me in one mouthful either.

Zephyr appeared to have an idea, however. He turned

to face the dog and, in a similar manner to a happy canine, lowered his front half and opened his mouth, tilting it to one side and sticking his tongue out.

At the same time, he lifted his back half up a little and waved his large swishing tail back and forth in the air.

This seemed to work. Roger let out a delighted-sounding yip at the playful body language universal to its kind and rushed closer. Zephyr kept still for the most part, his tail swishing back and forth until the dog was a lot closer and the group of humans with it had grown bolder.

"Hello," Zephyr said as the people came within only a couple yards, seemingly more interested in Roger and his reactions than they were the actual dragon before them. Not one of them jumped or looked surprised at hearing Zephyr speak.

"Do you often come down to the beach to have a bit of a frolic?" the woman asked, finally properly addressing Zephyr and I. Her words were calm, almost throwaway as if we'd been talking for a while and this wasn't the first thing she'd said.

"We fly over it mostly, but late at night, we run and exercise too," I replied.

"I like the way the moon reflects on the water," Zephyr said as Roger finally reached him and sniffed the dragon, his nose mere inches away from Zephyr's scales.

"Oh, I do too. I've always thought the night was more beautiful than the day. Mavis tells me I should get sleep while the stars are out, but I like them too much."

I laughed as the rest of the group grew bolder, finding myself in the middle of one of the strangest conversations I'd ever been part of.

The elderly men and women appeared to be having several conversations at once and didn't mind. And if a person wanted to switch from one to the other, they switched. It was three different subjects as well, and not all of them related.

Now and then, one even talked to themselves for a while before another person joined them.

Zephyr ingratiated himself with the dog owner, and they talked of star constellations and navigating by them while I talked with another subset about the rising prices and how it made life difficult right now.

It was like some elderly confab on random minutia, but instead of holding it in a café, we were having it in the middle of the beach with a dog, dragon, and myconid for company.

A yell from somewhere broke into my thoughts and made me lose my thread of conversation. I looked around, but it took me a moment to spot a woman with kids huddled near the top of the beach, a man coming toward us, striding and looking more than a little angry.

"How dare you," the man yelled.

"How dare I what? Have a conversation at the beach?" Mavis asked, her body stiffening, but his anger wasn't concerned with the old people. He looked at me instead, and I had a feeling I was now in for a rough ride.

"Not you, although I question your sanity, talking to such evil creatures. Dragons have been known to hypnotize and enslave people to meet their needs, promising long life and other bribes in return for worship and sacrifice," the man continued.

I stifled my sigh, but already I was wondering if we should leave. This kind of thing could get ugly fast.

"They're not evil. They can do some strange things, but that doesn't make them evil. You declare everything satanic if it's new and different! First it was the organ, then rock music, and now elves. Leave people in peace." The older folk continued to bristle, each of them coming to my defense in a way I hadn't expected.

The guy seemed to sense that it was a losing battle and spat on the sand instead.

Before he could walk off, however, and go back to his family, some other men came up, several of them swaggering and looking as if they were trying to start something.

"She bothering you?" the first one asked Mavis, flicking his head in my direction.

"Oh, no, she's been very kind. Even had her dragon friend help calm our dog. Have you seen the adorable little mushroom friend she has?" Mavis pointed at me, and Sen waved.

The men finally looked my way, the most shaved one stepping to one side so he could get a better look at Sen and me.

"What is that?" he asked.

"A dryad, of sorts." I smiled. "She's very friendly. Want to come say hi?"

The guy paused and I thought he was going to say yes, but the ringleader, a guy in a hooded sweatshirt and pants, practically growled.

"We don't want to meet scum like you. You killed our soldiers. Your kind should be herded up and shot."

"Good luck," I replied without thinking.

Immediately I regretted it, but no one seemed to be filming this altercation so far. It was a first.

"Look, I'm getting really tired of being threatened every time I go anywhere," I said while I had everyone's attention. "I'm here to get some fresh air and exercise. If that bothers you, go somewhere else and if it doesn't, great, we can all go on our merry ways."

Without giving anyone a chance to respond, I stalked off to my left, cutting across the front of Zephyr.

"It was nice to meet you all," I said to the group of elderly dog walkers, smiling at all of them. They got out of my way, but the thugs didn't seem to want to be done, and there were enough people on the beach that afternoon that we were beginning to draw a crowd. More and more were watching or approaching.

There was only one way out of this now and that was going to be flying away, but I was getting sick and tired of running from people. I stopped and looked around.

"Take your dragon somewhere it's wanted," a woman yelled, moving toward the young men who were still trying to swagger across the sand after us. The elderly also started walking, coming with me as well.

"It *is* wanted," I heard one of them say. "I was hoping to stroke those shiny scales. I could have told June about it when I visited her later."

Instantly I stopped. I turned back to him as I contemplated asking Zephyr if he'd mind, but I didn't know if I could do so. Zephyr wasn't a pet.

I'm good with him doing that, Zephyr said into my head. *I might not be a pet but to all these people I'm a wonder and touching something that you don't understand. Getting closer to it and being able to make some kind of memory about it—that's concrete and real. It's worth that.*

I nodded and tried to think of what I wanted to say. I had silence, and I intended to use it.

"I didn't ask for any of this. Just over a year ago, I was a waitress, and I was living a normal life in LA. Then I was practically given a dragon egg. I've done nothing but protect a misunderstood creature and stop mysterious people trying to kill me. And you know what, I don't regret it. I don't regret sending a message to whoever keeps attacking me and my kind."

While I spoke, I started to make the wind around me and the majority of the group swirl, careful to avoid actually blasting any person with sand, even weaving it between some of them.

"If I truly wanted to hurt people who were no threat to me, I could kill every last one of you, and there would be nothing you could do to stop me. You could pull a gun or call the cops, and still you would all die. And that's just what *I* can do. Both creatures with me are also powerful."

At this, Zephyr lifted his head and roared as loudly as he could. Some of the closest people covered their ears with their hands, and even I wanted to, but I kept my features calm and didn't react.

"But I don't want to do that," I continued. "I don't want to hurt anyone. So, unless you want to actually be civil, come see what a dragon scale feels like, meet a dryad, or chat to me about how I use magic, you can all piss off my area of the beach. Does everyone understand me?"

As I asked the last question, I lifted my hands and made the air whip around in the same pattern, and then I lifted the sand I could control into snowman-like structures, each one the height of someone angry at me and not far from them.

"Anyone stupid enough to keep yelling bullshit at me?" I asked again.

No one spoke, and I saw a few of them gulp.

"Good," I said as I cut my powers immediately, stopping the air for a fraction of a second while commanding all the sand to fall back to the beach. "Now, maybe we can all have a pleasant chat."

The younger males with far too much swagger than sense walked away, their leader quick to do so, and this seemed to take any fight out of the others as well.

I sighed as the elderly folk approached again.

"Who wanted to tell their June what I was like?" Zephyr asked as he hunkered down a little again and lowered his head. One of the men came forward, holding his wrinkled and thin hand up a little as he did.

"June's my wife. She's in a care home not far from here. I go see her every afternoon. She'd love to know I met you. When she was at her best, she used to read all sorts of fantasy stories."

"Why don't you get a picture with me?" Zephyr said, grinning as he did. "And let us know where the care home is. If we can, we'll pay her a visit."

"You'd do that?" he asked, looking at me.

"Why not? Sounds like it could be fun," I replied, grateful something good might come of this whole thing.

We needed some good PR. I could only hope the interview we'd just done would help.

For now, however, another crisis had been averted, and we were outside talking to people on the beach. I was starting to really wish we didn't get heckled everywhere we went, however.

CHAPTER TEN

When I saw Minsheng's face, I knew something was wrong. He had a frown fixed in place, and his breakfast sat untouched in front of him.

"What?" I asked as Zephyr went over to the fridge and pulled it open with his teeth.

Sen leaped onto a shelf and grabbed a package of sausages before springing back. I found a frying pan and moved to the stove, but I glanced a couple of times at my Shishou.

"That interview you did has come out. It was heavily edited, and..." Minsheng's voice trailed off as he shook his head. I paused, my stomach becoming a hard mass that wanted to weigh me down. If I hadn't been next to the kitchen counter, I think I'd have collapsed. As it was, I stepped toward the nearest chair and sat down.

"Show me."

Minsheng pulled out his phone, the video already up on the screen, and pressed play.

It was only about twenty minutes long after they'd cut

it down, but the whole thing had been cherry-picked, and it made me sound both violent and arrogant. By the time I had finished watching it, I was in tears. Was this really how the world was going to see me?

Daisy had come in before the end, and she put her arm around me.

"I'm sorry, Aella," she said. "This wasn't the kind of interview we hoped it would be. Chris is already seeing if he can get a hold of the full footage to release it all and show she manipulated this version of it."

I sighed as I nodded. This was the worst possible outcome, even if my friends could get the actual interview out there. There was always a subset of people who saw the first cut and never the second. On top of everything else, it was just confirmation that I was going to be judged and found wanting yet again.

While Daisy took over cooking breakfast for Zephyr, Sen, and me, I tried to think of ways we could actually combat this situation. Interviews clearly weren't working, but there wasn't a lot else I could think of.

To make matters worse, I had more of them booked.

"They're live ones, which will prevent the same thing happening twice," Minsheng pointed out, but it didn't make me feel much better.

Sensing my distress and what this might mean for us, Zephyr came close and rested his head on my lap. I stroked it as Sen ran along his body and jumped onto my shoulder as well. She then snuggled into my neck.

Immediately I felt sorry for the small dryad. She'd been happy in her forest until I'd come along and dragged her into a mess. It wasn't very kind of me to have done that to her. Could I possibly remove our bond and let her go back to her home?

Sen stay, her gentle voice said, reminding me that she could feel my concern for her as well. It made me feel a little better. At least my bonded creatures cared about me and wanted me to keep going.

We all have to continue and find a way through this, Zephyr thought. *There's a lot of mythicals counting on us, even if they don't know it yet.*

I knew he was talking sense, but a part of me didn't want to hear it. I'd had enough of being the one to take the hit when everyone else used my strength only when it suited them and then stood back and watched me take the heat for it.

It didn't help that people had reacted badly to the beach incident when I'd told them. As Minsheng had pointed out, I'd used my power to make them fear me, not respect me, and that was wrong.

Sighing, I was about to get up when Crawley and Emily came into the room, both also seeking their first meal of the day. Daisy quickly offered to sort them something as well, and they joined us at the table as Minsheng hurried off to prepare the day's training equipment.

As Crawley sat, I decided I couldn't let my previous request to the ex-agent lie with a negative response, but how did I persuade her to help me?

"I need you to reconsider my request," I said a moment later, deciding to be blunt.

She exhaled, looking up from the book she'd been reading. Our eyes locked, both of us trying to work out where the weakness was.

"It would make a difference if you told the public that I was often attacked for no other reason than that I existed."

"I know," Crawley replied, the first to look away. "But I can't do it. While I want to help you make the world a safer place for mythicals so this fighting stops and it's safer for Emily, this is a step too far. The agency has largely let me be here with you without causing too much trouble, but they're not going to tolerate it if I come out publicly in support of you."

"They wouldn't even exist anymore if you gave me the advantage I need to shed light on their practices. The human race would be accepting of us if they weren't constantly being made to feel afraid of me and as if the agency is justified. You could hand that to us."

"No," Crawley replied, shaking her head, but the gesture was resigned, sad. A hopeless refusal. "There's no guarantee it would do those things. I can't take the risk. I've helped you as much as I can. My daughter and I have paid for it. I understand if my refusal means you'd like us to leave, however."

I saw her glance toward her daughter and instantly shook my head. There was no way I was going to kick them out for not doing something risky for them. As much as I didn't want to accept it, Crawley was right.

We've still got things to try, Zephyr said. *And there's always the benefit of time. We'll find Jacobs, and then we can pay him a visit.*

A smile crept across my face at the thought of Zephyr finding Jacobs and having one of his chats with the man. Not that long ago, Jacobs had sent a sniper after us. We'd captured the man and, before calling the cops, we'd dangled him off a roof. He'd been safe enough, but of course, he hadn't known that. It wouldn't have surprised me if Zephyr wanted to do something similar to Jacobs himself.

Finished with breakfast, we went back through to the reception, but before we could go all the way up to the dojo and begin training for the day, we came across Iris and Minsheng, both of them noticing me immediately.

"Oh, there you are," Iris said, but she didn't sound pleased to see me.

The last time I'd seen her, she had been behaving all matronly over three gnomes we'd rescued not far from here after putting Zephyr and me through our paces. It had been a tough day, but she'd granted our request for funding to pay for the extension to the warehouse, and she'd even advocated for me to get a wage since then.

Her stern expression and set jaw as she looked me over and settled her eyes on Sen made me wonder why she was here today, however.

"Come to see the building progress?" I asked, hoping that was why.

"No. That appears to be progressing as expected. Behind schedule, but not so much the organization is worried. No, I am here because of recent events and the attention you appear to be getting and fostering."

"Great," I replied, not even trying to hide the sarcasm.

"I suggest you adopt a better tone and the four...five of us, find somewhere more private to have a discussion on the future of this little arrangement. Shall we?" Iris motioned to the stairs, but I wasn't sure where we could go that would be considered private enough.

Minsheng gave me a resigned look and led the way up with Zephyr not far behind.

Want me to dangle her off the roof too? Zephyr asked as we climbed the stairs, his body only just fitting around the bend.

I have a feeling it would only be fun for a moment. We'd have to put her down safely again somewhere, and she'd go straight back to the organization and terminate everything.

If only we didn't need her money.

One day we won't, I thought, almost as much promising myself as giving myself hope. We definitely needed to find a way to make more money ourselves.

Don't humans have sponsors for things sometimes? Zephyr suggested a moment later.

They do, but who is going to sponsor us? All we do in humanity's eyes is run a dojo where we teach mythicals how to fight and then stir up trouble whenever we go into the outside world.

Good point. We'll have to find another way to pay for more pizza.

I smothered the grin I wanted to give as Minsheng led us into his bedroom. It was a little bit smaller than mine, but if Zephyr curled up on the bed, we all could just about squeeze inside.

Sitting down on the floor in front of him, I finally gave Iris my attention again.

"Now, Minsheng here has already explained that today's interview was an unfortunate combination of being badly cut and not ever aired live."

"Yeah, we're trying to get the full thing to put it out there," I replied, sounding a bit like a whiny teenager getting all defensive and trying to point out what I had done about the problem.

"Yes, well... It's in the organization's best interests to aid with this, so I will be making my recommendation that we do so. After all, you've clearly tried where that one was concerned. However, we're growing alarmed by the interactions you're having with the public. Most appear to be finding their way onto social media."

"They do, but I always do my best with those as well. Not everyone starts out wanting to be friendly. And I refuse to let anyone push me around."

Iris pursed her lips, and I got the impression I shouldn't have been trying to justify anything.

I stifled my sigh and waited for her to speak.

"You have a task ahead of you that will require the support of every race on this planet. You cannot afford to injure any humans, even if they don't understand you."

More than don't understand us. They tried to arrest me and cart me off just for wanting potato chips, Zephyr said into my head, his tone of voice making it clear he was getting frustrated himself. I was pretty sure I heard him swish his tail around as well.

Iris glanced his way, and her eyes went wider before she regained her composure.

"I want you to stop fighting and showing off. You need to find a way to persuade all these people that you're friendly, and I don't think you're taking that task very seriously. You're acting like a recluse unless it suits you, and when you do go out, you act like everyone should get out of your way."

"Whoa. Back up there," I replied, knowing I was cutting

her off, but I wasn't about to listen to someone trying to claim I wasn't even trying to get along. "Every single time we've gone out lately, I've made friends and then someone else has come along and tried to sabotage whatever we've been trying to do."

"And then you've attacked them, making it clear people are either nice to you and Zephyr or they get the brunt of your abilities."

"No," I replied, beginning to really feel angry. "I've not attacked anyone at any point. I've merely defended myself, and I won't stop doing so. It might be hard to go out right now and not have some kind of altercation, but I refuse to hide in this building long-term, and I refuse to let people drive me away from a location because of their intolerance."

"Well, the organization is insisting you withdraw from those situations going forward." Iris folded her arms across her chest and Minsheng opened his mouth as if to suggest something, but I didn't want to hear it.

"Or what?" I demanded. And now I knew I sounded confrontational and whiny, but I was beginning to get sick of this. I'd been pushed around ever since I'd got to the Sanctuary and I was getting sick of it.

"Do I need to remind you that the organization is paying for all this?"

"No, but you might want to ask yourselves why, and while you do that, have a good think about whether you want to make me an enemy. Because that's what threatening me will do."

"Now, this is exactly what gets you into trouble—"

"No. This is who I am. I'm the defender. The champion.

Whatever you want to call me. That's what you all believe, isn't it? That I'm some sort of savior."

"There is a prophecy that the organization follows, and so far, you fit the relevant criteria," Iris replied as she adjusted her spectacles and fidgeted. She straightened her spine, still not backing down, however.

"Well, a defender defends. A champion fights for justice, and a savior saves those weaker and stands up to bullies. You can't come in here and demand I don't do those things because it rocks the boat. Saviors aren't loved by everyone. Leaders aren't respected by all they lead, and champions are often attacked by those who misunderstand them."

"Well, it's been known to happen—"

"I don't plan to stop. So either you decide to keep the money coming or you don't, but I don't answer to you. I answer to Zephyr and Sen. I answer to Minsheng. I answer to my conscience, and I answer to the myriad of mythicals out there who need me to stand up for them and make people think twice about harassing us."

Iris gaped, but I didn't stop there.

"While I don't intend to ever pick a fight, we're all in agreement that I need to change tactics. We'll be doing this our way, and trying to convince me otherwise is wasting all our time. Now, if you'll excuse me, we've got to train because apparently, the fate of the entire world rests on our shoulders."

Without another word, I stormed out, Zephyr following with Sen still riding on the top of his head.

As I stomped back down to the dojo, I calmed. It hadn't been the best idea of mine to yell at the person giving me money and paying for my new bedroom, but it had made me feel a lot better.

You know she was right about us needing to avoid fights where we can, though, Zephyr said as I became rational again.

I know. No more going out in broad daylight and scaring people.

No. It wasn't our finest moment. No matter how tempting.

So we'll go out at night and hide in the shadows again for a while, I replied, a part of me just fine with that idea. We'd said it before, but I'd always been tempted to ignore it. Operating entirely at night was hard.

Going to the cupboard, I picked out a bow and some arrows, intending to practice and finish growing calm enough to train more carefully with Sen and Zephyr.

Before I could fire the first arrow, Ronan appeared and joined me.

"Is it worth heading to the Sanctuary for a while?" he asked as we both shot. "It would give you some time to learn about your new abilities, give the council more time to adjust to this latest development, and we could take the pressure off here. If humanity knows you're not here, Lyra can operate more peacefully."

Letting out a sigh, I thought about my response. It was clear that Ronan had heard the heated argument I'd had. His room was next to Minsheng's. And he was truly trying to help.

"Okay," I replied. "Let's go find out what the masters can teach us."

CHAPTER ELEVEN

As the dawn sun came up and lit up the Sanctuary around us, I couldn't help but smile.

Good morning, sleepyhead, Zephyr said into my head, his gaze already turned on the world ahead of us, the sun beginning to shine on it. The sun was rising behind us, but it was still beautiful to see the sky change colors, growing lighter and gliding through the hues of an orange dawn.

We'd traveled through the early night to get to the Sanctuary, arriving an hour or so after midnight, Ronan and Erlan choosing to come with us this time. Minsheng had almost come as well, but he'd opted to stay and ensure Iris didn't actually stop our funding. At least until after the building work was complete, anyway.

Slowly I stood up, careful not to disturb Sen. She was curled up on Zephyr's back, near his wings, and looked adorable.

This view makes coming here worth it already, Zephyr said into my head a moment later.

I'm sure the training will be good too. I feel like we grow closer when we're here, and the masters help us work together.

They understand our bond better than Minsheng. He's not an elf.

No, but I wouldn't have anyone else as our Shishou.

Me neither. I just... Zephyr's mental voice trailed off, his emotions clouding my mind. I stepped closer and leaned into him, resting my head against his as I looped one arm over his neck and shoulders.

Here they treat you as another mythical, and out there they treat you like a beast I ride into battle, I suggested.

Yes.

I sighed, feeling the way he did about it, our bond letting me experience his emotions as he stopped even trying to hide them. If I was hurt that people kept treating me differently because of the way I looked, it was a thousand times worse for Zephyr.

I'm sorry, I thought. *I've not helped. Sometimes I've even made it worse.*

I think I have to be the one to fix it. We need to show me talking more when we go back to the human world.

We need to work together better too. I've been focusing too much on learning my new earth abilities. I'm neglecting our bond too much.

Our bond won't deteriorate while we work on other things. We're still using it every day, just in different ways.

I looked to Zephyr and smiled, reaching a hand to stroke some of the shiny scales. Once more, I marveled at how soft and sleek they felt, when in truth they were so hard they were bulletproof.

It was a reality I was also eternally grateful for. The

natural armor had saved his life many times and my own more than once. I didn't doubt that they'd protect us again in the future.

We stayed that way, watching the world brighten together until Sen also woke, the small dryad quick to get to her feet and spread her mushroom top out underneath the sunlight. I grinned as she appeared to power up in the sun, drinking it in.

A few moments later, we were also eating breakfast from the communal kitchens and greeting elves we knew and recognized.

Gwaelon, a water elf of great power in the Sanctuary, soon came up to us and plonked himself down with a bowl full of porridge and honey.

"Aella, my child. It is good to see your face here again. The mermaids tell me that you plan to stay a little longer this time."

I didn't know how to respond at first. Although I'd not made a secret of being back for a while and formally asked for somewhere we could stay for a week or so, I hadn't gone out of my way to talk to everyone yet. I'd also not seen the mermaids since the city had moved. It wasn't as if there was much in the way of water in this place.

"We diverted a stream and made a few pools for them to relax in. There's a good view from there," Gwaelon explained, practically reading my mind.

"Nice," I replied, and I meant it. He'd just told me that he and other elemental elves had changed a river and possibly the mountain to make a new habitat.

It made me wonder how much of the wilderness was truly wild and how much had been actually crafted that way by an elf who had needed something different at some point in the past. The whole world as it currently stood could easily have been made exactly the way it was.

I don't think elves have been that widespread, Zephyr said. *Very few of my memories are in a time where they weren't hiding.*

Sadness swept through me, and at first I thought it was coming from Zephyr, but then I realized it was from Sen, although all of us felt it. I tried to comfort her, and an image of a lush green forest came into my head as if it were my own memory.

In it, a young male elf was tending the forest, his touch enough to make bushes and flowers take on an extra vibrancy. It was beautiful.

Reaching for Sen, I tried to ask who the elf was, but I had a feeling now wasn't the right time.

A moment later, I looked up from my empty plate to realize that Gwaelon was staring at me, a grin on his face.

"Sorry," I replied. "We're still adjusting to the new extra bond and how it changes the way we communicate."

"Oh, don't be sorry for the delightful experience you're having. It has been a long time since an earth elf has bonded with a dryad, and we already know how much more special it is with you for other reasons. I can't wait to see what creature you bond with when you access the water aspect of your powers." Gwaelon sat back, looking as if he was thinking, and I was grateful.

That he thought I was going to automatically bond with yet another creature at some point threw me. I wanted time to adjust to the bonds I had and how they'd changed our dynamic. But I glanced at my companions and saw Sen happily sitting on the back of Zephyr's head again, some kind of cup and drink at her feet, her roots stretching into it.

Zephyr's look said everything. He was more than happy to have the dryad resting on him and enjoying her breakfast. And if anything, our strange little family had just grown bigger.

"What about a pegasus? If it was going to be one of the merpeople here, that would probably have happened already. I think you've begun using the water element, just slightly, on the edge of your consciousness." Gwaelon didn't look at me as he spoke, clearly thinking. "Then there's a kraken. That would be a formidable mythical to bond with."

My mouth fell open, not sure whether to query the existence of a kraken or ask how a pegasus was a water creature.

"You look confused. You've not met a kraken, have you?"

"No," I replied, laughing. "I'm not sure how I'd even begin to meet a large octopus that used to drown ships."

"Only in the myths the humans tell," he replied.

"Good point."

"Not confused about a kraken then. Which one surprised you?"

"The pegasus. In the myths I know, the pegasus is a flying horse of some kind. It should be an air elemental creature, shouldn't it?"

Gwaelon let out a small chuckle, but he didn't appear to be mocking me. "All the creatures can bond with any kind of elemental elf, because all of them have the capacity to adapt. For example your dryad. There are water dryads or sprites. And there are forest dryads of various types. There are even fire sprites and wind sprites."

"So there are water pegasuses?"

"Exactly. Have you ever heard tales of people seeing horses in the waves?"

"Yes, actually."

"That's a pegasus. A horse that's as much water as it is a horse. It can run anywhere the water can, and both bear weight and let the weight pass through it."

"Wow," I replied, feeling my mind being blown yet again. What if I bonded with something else? What if it was a kraken?

"Anyway, we had best get to training. I believe the masters are keen to have you in their lessons again." Gwaelon got to his feet and walked out of the eating area. I hastily followed after checking Sen was done, but she seemed to be in a serene trance, lying on her back on Zephyr and staring dreamily up at the sky.

Is she okay? I asked Zephyr, feeling for her with my mind and not detecting much of anything.

I think she ate too much. She's...digesting.

That was new, but I couldn't worry about how accurate that description was. I needed to get to lessons.

Here, the masters had made one of the caves near the surface of the network their training area. It had several openings and even a section of cave where the sun shone in, but it was still barely big enough for Zephyr.

At least, I thought so. I was just about to apologize to Zephyr when the air master spotted us and reached out to usher us in a slightly different direction to most of the rest of the elves. Wondering what they had in mind, I followed. It looked like we were heading deeper into the cave network.

After turning around several tunnels that also headed up, we came out onto a ledge under the sunlight. In this alcove of the Sanctuary, there was even more room for Zephyr, and we could also see the rest of the classes.

I grinned and thanked the kind elf.

"Oh, I'm not the one to thank for this. Orthelo worked out this was here and made sure we thought of you coming in to train. It's only right that we accommodate you as best we can. And this seemed ideal for your mix of abilities."

I nodded, and we spent the next ten minutes or so talking over all of my progress and the useful things we'd been practicing. I demonstrated a few things, Zephyr and I flying out and lifting Sen with us.

There wasn't much that combined my powers, however, but I mentioned the recent development and the way I was now combining abilities to fire projectiles with a lot more precision.

"Yes, I can see how that would make them more effective. You're controlling both elements at the same time."

"I wish I could suggest something I'd like to learn that isn't used in battle right now, but I fear another large fight is coming, and I wish to learn how to defend us as much as possible."

Before the air master could respond, I heard the clip-clop of a centaur's hooves on the cave floor and turned to see Ronan there. He'd come with me to the Sanctuary and had two bows and quivers with him.

I raised my eyebrows as he removed one of his bows and one of the quivers and held them out to me.

"I worked with the Sanctuary to place small targets about the mountainside and training caves," he explained. "You'll need to work with your companions to target them all."

Grinning, I reached for the air and rock around me with my mind, not sure how I'd want to control it but prepared to do so anyway. I reached for the first arrow and floated it into my hand. It was a little showy, but it amused me.

"I'll time you and check you've got them all," Ronan said as the air master returned to the rest of the class.

I felt a pang of desire to go join the others because I'd so often trained alone, but I suspected working alone was going to be my future. I was simply a lot more powerful than the other elven students. What challenged them was easy for me, and everything I was learning to do they were a long way off.

Taking a deep breath, I opened my mind to my companions more fully.

You both ready? I asked, not sure what we'd be facing, but knowing that if Ronan said we needed to work together, we needed to work together.

Always ready, Zephyr replied, his mouth open in a scaly grin.

Sen ready. The myconid jumped up onto Zephyr's head again and hunkered down as if she was holding on.

With both of them prepared to move and Zephyr's wings slightly extended, I looked at Ronan and nodded.

After a brief pause while he pulled out a stopwatch, he gave me a nod.

"Go," he said. Zephyr flapped into the air, and I used the air to blast upward. I came forward off the ledge, one hand holding my bow and arrow as Zephyr launched.

Almost immediately, I spotted a small red and white circular target attached to the side of the ledge we'd been standing on. I twisted and allowed myself to fall several feet. Steadying myself, I hovered and shot the arrow I carried.

It hit the target, but it was more than a little off-center.

Trying not to worry too much, I powered back up and looked for the next, only to find one at the top of the cave. Zephyr beat me to it. Almost flipping over, Zephyr flew up and grabbed it with a claw, crushing it. Chunks of wood broke off and went flying.

I steadied the pieces so they didn't hit the other elves below us and carried on, heading toward the sky exit of the caves above the ledge. I could feel Zephyr not far behind.

Although Sen had held on fairly well as Zephyr had turned almost entirely upside down, she leaped my way as I came closer and managed to land on my shoulder. Her root-like feet gripped me, and her arm wrapped around some of my hair.

Just as we burst out of the cave, I noticed another red target. This one was almost buried in the rock, the reflection of it visible in a small pool of water that sat in the bottom of a dip.

I came closer, trying to move my body around to get an angle where I could see it to hit directly. There were just too many rocks protruding, however. No matter how I helped my arrow fly, it wouldn't get to the target.

Sen help, the dryad said as she jumped from my shoulder over to the gap and then ran along it, just small enough that she could fit. She took a rock with her and hurled it at the target as soon as she had a clear view.

The reflection showed me a hit before she came scurrying back, her body springy and fast for one so small.

I flew closer to the gap, but she jumped back over to me before I could reach out, gripping onto me once more and turning herself as I powered up again. Zephyr was in the sky above us already, his gaze darting from left to right.

Another target fifty yards dead ahead of you, he said into my head as he dived for another to my right. Spotting what he meant, I lifted until I had another good angle and fired down upon it.

I almost missed but remembered to use my powers to help direct the arrows just in time. I corrected its course and impaled the target before coming up again to look for more.

Before I could react, something came flying toward me, but Zephyr was already moving and diving between us, and whatever it had been, it bounced off his scales with a thud.

Sen attack, she said a moment later. *Go down.*

I obeyed, not sure what she'd spotted, but I darted back down and let her jump into a tree nearby. She then flipped and jumped her way down to the lower branches before springing to the ground and into a run.

While Zephyr lifted up again to try and spot more

targets, I did the same, my eyes still darting back to Sen occasionally as she ran at some kind of strange bush.

A moment later, it flicked a branch, and another large gray object flew at me. This time I was able to slow it with my powers and hold it in the air until I could get to it.

As I took it in my hands, I realized it was a strange cross between a mango, a melon, and a peach, but gray. It also smelled disgusting. I had a feeling it wasn't something I'd want to hit me.

When I spotted my next target, I threw it at that instead, then Sen returned out of the bush, several branches in her hands, teeth marks on either end of each bit of wood. I landed and picked her up as Zephyr did the same, spitting out another target.

Ronan appeared, his strong legs bringing him out of an opening in the rock just wide enough for his body.

He looked at the damage we'd done to the targets outside and frowned.

"I expected you to go on the offensive, but I didn't expect you to wreck the entire setup," he said.

"Sorry. We got carried away," I replied, but I could hear Zephyr chuckling, and Sen was grinning and prodding another strange gray fruit with her stick.

Ronan shook his head, but he also smiled. It looked like we'd gotten away with it.

CHAPTER TWELVE

I sighed as I finished saying my last goodbye. We'd been at the Sanctuary for a week, and now it was time to head back to the dojo and my warehouse. We still needed to keep a low profile, so we had set out a few hours after darkness had fallen. Erlan and Ronan were both ready to head home, and I was more than in need of getting back to LA.

While it was great to be at the Sanctuary and to train with people who understood what it felt like to wield magic the way I did, it was strange not being with Minsheng and away from all the technology and everything else that came with the human world.

Can we get pizza when we get back? Zephyr asked, making it clear he'd missed a few human comforts as well.

If we get back before the good takeaway place shuts, I replied, knowing we probably would. Even with having to travel slower so Erlan and Ronan could come with us, the Sanctuary wasn't as far from the dojo anymore. It was also high up in a mountain so we'd be going downhill most of the way. Ronan could cover a fair few miles, carrying Erlan most of the way.

Minsheng was meeting us on the outskirts of LA, where we wouldn't be able to travel on the ground without being seen, and once he had Erlan and Ronan safe, Zephyr, Sen, and I could fly wherever we wanted.

It felt a little strange to be in the air and flying low, so we could see Ronan. To make it easier for me to pinpoint them, Sen was also riding with them, her extra weight almost negligible.

She wasn't completely happy about not getting to fly, but we needed safety and good communication over other options.

As the Sanctuary faded into the distance behind us, the night obscuring it from view, I felt a pang of sadness as well. I was becoming so torn between the two locations, never entirely wanting to leave either but always yearning for something the other provided.

It was impossible to choose between them for so many reasons. But at some point, I feared I was going to have to. They weren't quite close enough for me to keep up the traveling, and the mythicals in LA needed me often enough that I had to go back regularly.

We'd been traveling for half an hour when Ronan slowed and started to fall behind.

What's wrong? I asked Sen as Zephyr slowed too, possibly feeling the same tug I did at having the distance increase between us and our bonded mythical.

Men, Sen replied, feeding me an image but no sound.

Agents came blurrily into view, a group of four of them seemingly patrolling an area.

Ronan backed up as we flew around the patch, Zephyr already identifying where they were and reducing the distance between us. If the agents attacked them, I wanted to be close to the others to help defend and get them to safety.

I tried to spot the agents with my own eyes, but I still couldn't find them among all the trees. Sen was the only one who could as Ronan started to head around them.

They didn't appear to be doing a very good job of keeping a watch out, three of them opting to sit down. They looked like they were talking, but I couldn't hear what they were saying through our bond.

When the fourth appeared to notice Ronan and suddenly stared in Sen's direction, I frowned. Although a huge part of me wanted to attack and take out all four agents, I didn't want them to be sure they'd found us this close to the Sanctuary.

We needed a diversion.

Thankfully I still had my new bow and arrows strapped to my back, and I quickly pulled them off as Zephyr flew us closer. With any luck, it would disturb a few birds and make enough noise that the men started looking in the other direction while Ronan continued to get farther away.

Taking very careful aim and using my powers to help it fly true, I shot an arrow over the agents' heads and into the base of a nearby tree.

It flew straight and true, the *thunk* it made as it hit the tree audible from where I was. IThe men turned and one of them stood again, giving Ronan the opportunity to slip even farther away.

Zephyr continued to fly circles, keeping away from the

moonbeams as Ronan picked up speed and got himself, Erlan and Sen a safe distance away. Once he was farther out from them and heading away again, we flew after them, staying low to keep an eye on our friends for a little longer.

Only when the agents were long behind us did I relax. Although I was curious about why they'd been there and what they'd been up to, I didn't have the time to stop and take them on. I was also supposed to be keeping a low profile.

Despite that, I had a few nagging doubts. Could they have been hunting down other mythicals? If so, I hadn't seen any. It was also possible they were looking for orbs still, but I was pretty sure they weren't near one. That left me with no strong reason for their presence.

Could they have been looking for us? Zephyr asked, his thoughts gentle as if he'd just thought of the idea himself. I had no way of knowing, but now he'd suggested it, the thought wouldn't go away.

What if they were looking for us?

We should keep a lookout and make sure they don't follow us, I replied. *And we should let Ronan know to be careful.*

Ronan watching, Sen replied.

For now, it was the best we could do. Keep heading home but be more aware of trouble.

Twenty minutes later, I noticed there was a deep throbbing coming from our right and behind somewhere. It sounded like a helicopter, and it was coming closer. It wasn't long before I thought I heard another somewhere ahead.

Coincidence? I asked Zephyr before lifting up off his

back, using my powers to propel my body up and forward.

I don't think so.

How have they found us?

The previous set of agents probably communicated with some others. Especially if they found your arrow. And we're heading somewhere expected.

Good point. I swooped down toward Ronan and landed near him, getting his attention.

"Company in the skies," I said quietly, the sound of helicopters obvious on the ground as well. "Might need to get you and Erlan somewhere safe and out of the way while we deal with them."

Ronan frowned but nodded.

"We'll call you if we get separated," Erlan replied, flashing the burner cell he now sported.

I gave him a grin as Sen jumped to my shoulder. With Zephyr still in the sky, I pushed the air outwards and hurled myself upward again.

Immediately Ronan ran off with Erlan, and I was left with Zephyr.

We should try and deal with them one at a time, Zephyr said, hanging back.

I considered suggesting we take on one each, but I had a feeling Zephyr was right and we were going to need to work together. Given we'd stopped for a while, I was also pretty sure the one behind us was closer, but Ronan was ahead, and I was worried about him.

Zephyr was already flying toward the sound behind us, however, and I noticed there were now also cars on the road nearby, far more cars than there should be for the quiet area and the roads we had chosen to travel near.

It made my mind up. There was a good chance the agency was going to try and pin us down.

As I came closer to Zephyr, however, something opened fire nearby, loud gun blasts disturbing the forest below.

Instinctively, I darted up and away from the noise and tried to solidify the air around me. A moment later, I felt a flare of pain inside me, and I heard Zephyr grunt.

You okay? I asked Zephyr, flying toward him and blasting air at the direction the noises were coming from.

They must be using some kind of different bullet or something else. They caught my underside, and I think they've drawn blood.

Anger filled me and I swooped back toward the danger, trying to see whoever had shot while reaching for the forest with my mind.

Sen attack, she said, the determination in her words more than I expected. Before I could stop her, she had leaped from my shoulder and into a tree below.

The helicopter arrived, and the cars pulled up. They'd somehow worked out where we were, and they were hunting us down. Another shot was fired, and I managed to spot the man shooting. He had a launcher over his shoulder, and it lit him up for just a moment.

Sen rushed straight for the man as Zephyr managed to dodge the attack meant for him again. A moment later, the helicopter opened fire on me.

Surprised it had even been able to see me, I pulled up as Zephyr flew across the bullet path, the projectiles bouncing off the hardened scales along his back before we rose together.

As Zephyr flew over the helicopter and came down the other side onto the tail, more noise caught my attention. Even more cars were pulling up, agents and what appeared to be soldiers rushing out.

I needed to do something to help, and fast. But as I caught sight of a camera, I could have sworn.

Don't hurt anyone, I yelled into both Sen and Zephyr's heads. *They're filming this. Trying to make us look like aggressors again.*

I threw up an air wall between the agents and me.

There was an almighty crack as Zephyr tore the tail off the helicopter and sent it spinning.

Can you catch it, Aella? he asked, his voice frantic. I whirled around, not entirely sure I could focus on three things at once. It was hard enough to keep myself in the air while forming a wall, but I had to try.

I focused on not letting the helicopter body fall first and then slowed the spin it was in, working hard while the agents continued to fire on me. I was vaguely aware of someone yelling something to the side, but I ignored it and slowly moved the helicopter pod over to the road before lowering it down to the ground.

Sen broke gun, I heard her say a moment later and then felt her running my way.

Moving myself lower as well, I could finally make out the person yelling although I still couldn't clearly hear what they were saying. It was too muffled and distorted.

Turning, I moved a little closer. An agent was standing on the top of one of the agency cars and some lights had been set up, almost as if I was deliberately being called forward.

Not sure what else to do, I slowly hovered closer, the air wall still there.

Stay out of sight, Sen, I said just to her as Zephyr flew down beside me, also facing the agents. *It's better if they don't think you're here.*

"Why did you attack me?" I yelled as loudly as I could.

"We'll defend our people against all aggressive actions," the guy with the megaphone said, his words finally clear enough for me to hear.

"Including whoever was launching grenades unprovoked against Zephyr?" I replied, still moving toward them and lower. Spotting an open patch the other side of them, I raced over and landed, making sure my air wall then swept around Zephyr and me.

The large dragon touched down beside me and I finally got a glimpse of his wound. It wasn't huge; some of the scales had been darkened by the blast, and a couple had been ripped off. It had to be hurting, however, and I could still feel a dull ache on my own torso as if I mirrored his pain.

I frowned before looking at the agents ahead of us again. Loads of them had guns trained on us, but none of them were shooting.

"I'll ask you all again," I said. "What were you planning to do about the man who launched a grenade at Zephyr? We were flying home. Nothing more."

"You attacked our helicopter. We will defend ourselves."

"Your people are unharmed despite firing on us. I suggest you back down. I have someone out there with a grenade launcher to track down," Zephyr said before roaring.

It took not just me by surprise but the men as well. They moved some of their guns from me to him.

"You're not going anywhere. We're arresting you for attacking a civilian."

"No, you're not," I replied. "I haven't attacked anyone but defended myself from a helicopter that opened fire on me."

"You attacked a man in the woods before we arrived."

I let out an exasperated growl. They were clearly trying to frame me. As I did, Zephyr moved, however, and came to stand right in front of me. He then bared his side to all the agents, his wound visible.

There were a few gasps, and even the agent with the megaphone lowered it. It was clear that they hadn't expected him to be injured, and it made me worry that we'd exposed a weakness they hadn't known about. Maybe having a weakness would make the general population more sympathetic toward us, however.

"We were flying home and were attacked," I said. "Your helicopter then joined in the assault. None of your agents are currently harmed. I suggest you all leave, and we'll go on our way."

"I'm sorry, we can't allow that," the guy with the megaphone said, thankfully not through the megaphone itself.

I stepped around Zephyr again, placed my hand on his shoulder, and surveyed what was before us. There were about twenty agents and they only appeared to have normal guns. Whoever had been using the grenade launcher, they were either pretending he wasn't one of them or he truly wasn't.

"I think we all know you can't stop me from leaving if I

want to. We also all know that this was a setup. Zephyr and I are going to leave now and return peacefully to our home. If you want to send someone to get a statement from me, you can. That's the best I'll offer. Goodnight."

With that, I pushed off and rose into the air, Zephyr flapping his wings and doing the same.

None of them fired, and we managed to get high enough I dared move to the side again. Although the agents weren't packing up just yet and heading home, I didn't move too far away. Part of me wanted to see what they did next, and the other part of me was worried about Sen.

I could feel her down in the forest not too far from them. She was already working her way toward me, but we weren't safe and reunited yet, and she couldn't run as fast as we could fly.

On top of that, I didn't know what she'd done to the guy with the grenade launcher. She'd broken his weapon so we were safe, but what about the wielder?

Then there were Ronan and Erlan. The second helicopter had never materialized. Had they been recalled while we took care of the first? That would have been a hell of a coincidence.

As Sen made it to a small clearing, Zephyr and I landed. The agents were far enough away that we could barely hear them if we were quiet. I wanted to check Zephyr's wound.

I'd noticed on prior occasions that if Zephyr got hurt, I felt some of the pain somewhere inside me, and this time it was no different. He was hurting so I was as well. Admittedly I was pretty sure it didn't hurt me as much as him, but it only made me worry that he was hurting a lot more.

Sen came close as well, resting one of her hands on Zephyr's giant leg as I used my phone as a flashlight to check the damage. The blood had dried and the wound had scabbed over, but it still looked nasty.

Only on the surface. The scales took the damage. It's no different from you losing skin. They'll grow back, Zephyr explained.

I suspected it wasn't quite the whole truth, but I had a feeling he wasn't going to confess to being in any more trouble than that. Before we could get in the air again, however, I saw the outline of a centaur with someone on his back, and Ronan and Erlan came into the clearing.

Relief flooded through me when I saw they were unharmed. Erlan slid off Ronan's back and came running over, his phone in his hand.

"I think I got it all," he said. "Well, almost all of it. All the bits that matter. Shall I put it on the internet?"

"Put what on the internet?" I asked immediately.

"The battle you had with the guy firing grenades, the helicopter and then that stupid conversation with the agents afterward," Erlan replied, smirking.

I didn't know how to respond, my mind struggling to process his confession that he'd captured the entire thing on camera from our point of view.

"Did you get the initial shot? The one that hurt Zephyr?"

Erlan nodded, the grin on his face getting even wider.

"Then yeah. Post it. Let the world see how the agency treats us."

CHAPTER THIRTEEN

As our home finally came into sight, I let out an exhausted breath and slowly let go of some of the air I'd been controlling, no longer helping Zephyr stay in the air as much.

Somewhere in the city, Minsheng was also driving Erlan and Ronan back. It was possible they'd already made it to the warehouse, but we had no easy way to tell.

After escorting Erlan and Ronan to the meeting point with my Shishou, we'd paused and Zephyr had rested for a bit while I ate. We'd kept to the shadows and then I'd fallen asleep, exhausted after the situation from earlier in the night.

Rather than waking me, Zephyr and Sen had simply kept watch and continued to rest themselves. I'd woken up only a couple of hours later, but the sleep had done wonders. We were becoming more nocturnal with everything that was going on, but my body was still adjusting to full nights of activity.

As we swooped down toward the warehouse, I saw that the building work had progressed significantly while we'd been away at the Sanctuary. In the end, we'd been gone just over a week, but it had been enough time for the builders to finish all the roofing and get all the windows in. The building was once more air-tight.

It was a relief all of its own. Once the rooms had all their internals installed, we could spread out a bit more, and no one would have to sleep in the changing rooms again.

No sooner had we entered the building than I saw Minsheng coming out of the small room he currently used. No one spoke; the rest of the warehouse inhabitants probably fast asleep. We didn't want to wake them.

He motioned toward the stairs with his head, and we willingly padded after him and down to the kitchen and dining area. Before I could suggest to Zephyr that we eat something, the takeaway long shut, Minsheng had turned the oven on and fetched several frozen pizzas from the chest freezer.

I gave Zephyr a grin before fetching Daisy's first aid kit. Even if Zephyr was going to continue being stubborn about his wound, I wanted to clean it and stick some kind of bandage over it for now.

While I tended to Zephyr, Minsheng got everyone a drink, starting with a bowl of plant food and water for Sen. She stuck her feet into it, sitting on the table surface as she did.

"Erlan and Ronan had quite a story to tell me," Minsheng said as he put two hot drinks down on the table, one of them clearly for me.

"Yeah. The agents don't appear to have given up on us,"

I replied. "And it looks like they're trying to drag what's left of my reputation through the mud as well."

I sighed as I cut a section of bandage big enough to cover Zephyr's lost scales. The patch was about as big as my hand once the scales beside it had been cleaned.

It also looked like a few of them were cracked and some more were singed. No wonder it had hurt.

"This can't keep happening," Minsheng said. "It's as if the battles we were having are now fights about who can leak footage of what disgraceful behavior and in which way."

"It definitely looks like that," I replied, but I hadn't needed Minsheng to point it out. I felt like I had no idea how to fight this kind of fight. This wasn't one where I could just smack someone in the face repeatedly or let Zephyr knock them out if they were irritating me. I had to somehow win the hearts and minds of people I didn't know without getting to meet them.

And it was clear I was sucking at it.

It's not the sort of battle any of us have ever faced before, Zephyr said into my head. *The internet didn't exist the last time I remember being a dragon.*

It was a good point. In battles I often relied on Zephyr's memory of strategy, tactics and tricks Tuviel and Azargad had used. In this new fight, none of us had any advantages.

Before either of us could move, there was a knock at the door. Given the time of night I was surprised, but I hurried toward it, Zephyr following in case I needed backup or someone somewhere was in danger.

It wouldn't have been the first time for someone to come to the door in need of immediate physical assistance to defend themselves from humans who didn't appreciate mythicals.

The person standing in the porch light wasn't someone mythical, however. It was an agent I recognized from the agency here in LA. Zephyr and I had gassed this man on more than one occasion. I was pretty sure I'd also broken his arm once, or something similar.

Slowly, I opened the door.

"What do you want?" I asked, my tone suspicious and far more unfriendly than I'd originally intended.

"Oh, to deliver a little surprise to you," the agent said, smiling and making me feel even more apprehensive. As he spoke he pulled an envelope from his jacket pocket and handed it over.

The envelope had my name on it and the warehouse address. Was this something to do with the earlier attack?

"Quite a few of the agents wanted to bring you this, but I was given the honor."

"Is it a request for a statement?" I asked, figuring it needed to be something similar if not that.

"I'm not going to spoil it. Open it. Do what you need to do and I look forward to the next time I see you." The agent's smile grew even wider but he didn't move, watching my reaction.

Frowning and keeping the door ajar, I tore the envelope open. Inside was a letter informing me that the US government was launching an official inquiry into me and my involvement in a large-scale attack on US soldiers and agents.

Of all the incidents I'd expected the letter to be about, it wasn't something that had happened over two months ago.

I'd expected them to want a statement or to be declaring that I had to set up a justice system with courts and everything that went with them so I could try mythicals for crimes.

It also said that I was going to have to appear in court tomorrow. Not exactly a lot of warning.

I looked up from reading it to see that the agent was still standing there, a grin on his face.

"Bit late for you to be delivering this, isn't it?" I asked.

"I work whenever I need to. The agency has noticed that a certain group of mythicals are active later and later, so we're also working later and later." The agent folded his arms across his chest as if he'd just scored a point against me.

"Well, good luck catching us in the pitch black."

"Oh, don't you worry about that. There's more than one way to see in the dark. See you in the morning. I'm looking forward to you having to explain yourself." The agent flashed me yet another grin before turning around and walking back to his car.

I knew I should have been angry that he'd come here so late at night and delivered me a court summons, but his last words had made sense of what happened earlier. They'd found a way to detect us in the dark.

Heading back to the kitchen, I found Minsheng was no longer alone. Chris had appeared. I quickly filled them in on what was happening.

I had to listen to them as they grew angry about the court summons. Although it bothered me as well, my mind was still elsewhere.

"I'll go to court in the morning, and we'll do what we

have to do. It's not the first time I had to explain in front of an audience what my actions were and why. I might need a lawyer, though."

"The organization will provide one. I should let them know," Minsheng replied.

"Before you do, there's one more thing. I managed to get the agent to brag a little, and he let slip that they've been tracking us or found a way to see us in the dark."

"I suspected as much when Minsheng told me what happened tonight. It's probably a heat-detection system." Chris sat back, looking thoughtful.

"It sounds like you already have some kind of idea on how we can solve that problem."

"It might need a little dwarven magic. But I think I might be able to come up with something. Leave it with me," Chris said as he grabbed a snack and left again.

Instantly I felt a little better. Chris and his gadgets had solved many of our problems. Making us invisible to a heat detector wasn't a small problem, but if anyone could solve it, he could.

"You should probably get some sleep," Minsheng said, his phone in his hand.

"I don't think I'll be able to sleep yet. I need to have an idea about what I'm going to say in court and if there's anything I should avoid talking about. It's not as if they've given us very long to prepare."

"I'm pretty sure that was the point." Minsheng glanced at the time, and I followed his gaze.

It was gone four. They probably hadn't expected to find me still up despite the agent's words.

"Phone the organization and let's get a lawyer here as quickly as we can. I'm also going to need a lot of caffeine."

With that, I sat down next to Zephyr. If Jacobs wanted to play these kinds of games, I wasn't going to just roll over and let him win. This was just another kind of fight.

Any memories that might help us? I asked Zephyr.

Court is new territory to me as well. Am I even going to be able to come in with you?

I have no idea. Maybe I can claim you're some kind of therapy pet. That's even assuming there's a door big enough to let you in.

Zephyr let out a sigh. A world that wasn't used to dragons was not a fun world for him to live in.

The organization acted quickly. I had to hand it to them; even though they weren't entirely happy with me right now, they were willing to defend me. Within half an hour, I had a message from a lawyer saying he was on the way.

"I'll make us all some coffee," Minsheng said as he showed the lawyer into the kitchen.

"Is there somewhere less public in the building that we could go?" the lawyer asked by way of an introduction.

I shook my head and got to my feet. The lawyer's eyes flicked to Zephyr and Sen.

Although I expected him to show some kind of fear at being in front of a dragon for the first time, to his credit, he stepped forward, looked Zephyr in the face, and extended his hand.

"You must be Zephyr. My name is Robert Johnson. I confess that this is going to be my first time representing a dragon, but I'm very pleased to meet you."

Zephyr slowly lifted his large claw, and being as gentle as possible, shook his hand.

"And that must make you the very, very famous Aella-Faye," he said as he turned his attention to me.

"I don't know about the very famous part," I replied, "but I'm Aella."

"Right, we should begin by you telling me the whole story in your own words. And I want you to start at the beginning, whatever that is to you. Can you do that?"

"I can try. But it doesn't begin where they say it does. It begins several hours earlier than the camera started rolling and in a different location altogether."

"Great. If it's all right with you, I'd also like to record this. It will help me prepare you to be able to listen to the way you phrase things again and work out if there's any better way to do it."

He glanced around, taking the coffee Minsheng offered him before looking at me again.

"I know this isn't the most ideal place to be talking, but this building doesn't really have many private spaces. Everyone here is part of our team, however. They're all mythical or allied with us entirely. Our fate is tied to theirs strongly enough that they'll not want to do anything detrimental. And I'm sure we can keep them quiet when they come in for breakfast."

Mr. Johnson smiled and nodded before putting his bag down. He quickly unpacked his stuff, getting out a pen, paper, and some notes. When the recorder was set up, he picked up his pen and gave me a nod.

After thinking back to the beginning of that night, I started talking. I told him how a mythical had gone missing and how we'd tracked her down to a government base in the middle of nowhere. How we'd gone into the base, knocking out agents until we'd found the missing mythical and her cell. How she'd been abused and tortured. And then how we'd freed her and learned that the majority of the agents and soldiers on the base were on their way to attack and kill everyone at the Sanctuary, a refuge for peaceful mythicals, and how we already had reason to believe it was true.

Over the next two hours I told him everything we'd done and why. That we'd tried to avoid deaths despite risking our lives. The nights of endless attempts to get into the Sanctuary. How we felt threatened, persecuted and bullied for no more than existing, and how our only wish was to live as free as any other American citizen.

Mr. Johnson's attention never wavered, his concentration fully on hearing me and making notes. It didn't seem to faze him when Zephyr spoke either. To him, this was another voice in the story. Another person to defend.

"Wow," he said when I finally finished speaking. "I suspected you'd had a reason to attack that convoy, but not something like this."

He took a deep breath and then looked at me again.

"Now we need to work out how to prepare you best," he said, rubbing his hand across his chin.

I nodded, waiting for him to think through whatever he wanted to say. He'd given me his undivided attention and respect and now I'd give him mine.

"This isn't as simple as it looks, but I think we should focus on the evidence you already had on how they'd treated the imprisoned mythical. It's huge that she was taken against her will and not charged with any crimes. That she hadn't committed any crimes and that you had evidence you believed that they were going to attack again. In your mind, you were acting to prevent war crimes. But that defense relies on them recognizing mythicals as a respectful entity. As a people."

"They are. I only acted to protect them from an attacker who had no right to do what they were planning to do. I believe all my actions were right."

"Morally, yes. But you're being investigated in the United States for breaking their rules. It's not the same thing. They don't care if it was the right thing to do, just if you broke their laws."

This was a truth that made me sigh. He had a good point. And it reminded me of a time in the past when I'd been angry about some high-profile case and the verdict the judge had given. A friend had pointed out that the result followed the law, but that didn't make it just.

The laws didn't always deliver justice.

"I want you to help me make the truth known and help people see that I acted in a manner I believed to be morally right, but I'm going to need you to help me not end up in a jail cell as well. While I do want to say my piece and I am willing to cooperate with this investigation, I have no intention of letting them put me in a jail cell. And if they decide I've broken a law of some kind, we're going to be butting heads in a whole new way."

"I thought you might say something like that," he replied, grinning. "Then let's begin. This isn't a normal case, exactly. For starters, you've not been charged, and this is just an investigation."

"So I don't have to tell them everything?"

"Technically, you don't need to do that even if you've been charged with a crime. You just have to answer questions. But in an investigation, it's different again. You don't technically have to even tell the truth. I won't advise that you lie, but no one can stop you from doing so."

"While I appreciate you pointing out the distinction, I don't intend to lie, just speak my piece."

"Noted," he said before spending the next hour telling me what he thought I should focus on and how and what I might want to leave out.

By the time he was finished, we'd drunk more coffee and had breakfast. Daisy and some of the earlier risers were up and about.

"I'd like to head back to the office and look a few things up, but I can meet you at the court in a couple of hours," Mr. Johnson eventually said as he got to his feet.

"Thank you," I said, feeling better prepared but still shattered.

As soon as he left, I asked Daisy to wake me in time for us to fly over to the court, and Zephyr, Sen, and I went to get as much sleep as we could.

CHAPTER FOURTEEN

Our destination loomed ahead, a grand building with press outside and plenty of people milling around in business suits.

Zephyr and I landed separately beside each other, Sen on my shoulder. I'd considered leaving her behind, but we'd decided it was better if she was with me.

As we'd expected, there was an immediate response to the building having a dragon on their front doorstep. The press also flashed photos of us as security came over, many of them looking nervous.

"I'm sorry, but you can't bring pets into the building," the first one said, making me roll my eyes and just turn to Zephyr. Why did everyone seem to think he was some kind of pet? He'd spoken so many times now.

"I'm not a pet," he simply said. "And where Aella goes, I go too. To separate us for a prolonged period of time is a murder sentence to us both."

The security guard nearest didn't seem to know how to

respond, but I saw our lawyer come over to us, a smile on his face.

"This way," he said. "I think Zephyr should be able to fit through if we go through the main door, although it might be a squeeze getting him into the room we're using."

"We can't allow a dragon into the building," the security guard protested again, his hand going to his holster and the gun that sat within.

"I wouldn't bother with that if I were you," I said, pointing to the weapon. "He's bulletproof, and my powers can send the bullet flying in another direction. It's probably best if we don't have one ricocheting off into the crowd and harming innocent people now, isn't it?"

Again the security men blinked and looked between each other.

The lawyer immediately took charge again, ushering the three of us toward the large double doors.

As we'd all predicted, it was a squeeze to get Zephyr inside and no one could walk past him while he was moving down the hallway, but my lawyer handled the situation with a great deal of grace and patience.

While he led us toward the room our investigation would be conducted in, other lawyers, judges, and people involved in cases being heard in the building opened doors to peek out and even took a step or two into the corridor toward us.

Each time Mr. Johnson waved them back, asking them to duck into side rooms or simply wait on the other side of the section we were traveling down. Thankfully the room we were using also had a set of double doors, although one was still locked in place.

The security on the door scrambled to unlock it and pull it open, their eyes wide and staring at Zephyr as he came closer.

I tried to be polite and say hi to everyone we passed, as did Zephyr, making even more of an impression. Most people said hello back, acknowledging the dragon with dignified surprise. Some seemed composed enough to hide their shock or maybe they were some of the few who realized he could speak.

Finally we entered the main room, and I saw rows of chairs and tables laid out in a square, several microphones placed on tables, and wires running through the open space in the middle.

There were already a handful of people in the room, and immediately there was a reaction to Zephyr's presence when he followed me through the door, having to pause with most of his tail and his back legs out in the corridor behind still.

"No, no, no. How did you get him past security?" a woman said, almost screeching. "Guards! Get him out of here."

"I'm sorry, but he needs to stay," Johnson said before we could protest and the few guards nearby could do more than gulp. "The dragon, and I believe the myconid on Aella's shoulder, are both bonded to her. They're a lot like one soul. We cannot separate them. If Aella is to attend this investigation and answer questions as she has been instructed, then they must be present as well."

"We will need proof of this. I'm not just taking your word for it."

I grinned. We'd been expecting this, but it had taken us

a while to decide how we'd prove we were bonded and something magical was happening.

"Do you have a piece of paper or something that you could show me, and only me?" I asked, stepping closer and leaving Zephyr by the door.

"Here, I do," Johnson said, picking up a piece of paper from one of the tables. It seemed to be some kind of schedule for the room. As I put Sen down on another table, I turned so my back was to Zephyr. I read the words in my head, being careful to focus on each one.

As I finished each sentence, Zephyr repeated it from behind me.

"That's the best way we can prove that we're linked like one. I have no desire to risk my death to show you anything further. Will this satisfy you?" I asked, holding my head just a little higher as I reached for Sen again. The myconid grinned up at me, making me smile back.

The woman's mouth had fallen open during the recital, but she snapped it shut.

"I still don't believe that his presence is necessary, and it's intimidating to the other people in the room, but I will allow him to remain."

"Why does he intimidate people," I asked, furious at the lack of respect he was getting, "yet I don't? You know I could kill you all just as quickly as Zephyr, right? I could do far more damage to the building as well. You fear him because you've been told dragons are monsters in stories, but he's the only one alive right now. And he's no more a monster than I am."

"There are plenty of humans who can kill more humans than me too," Zephyr added, although I felt him trying to calm me down, waves of peacefulness coming through our bond.

I took several deep breaths. I wasn't sure I was helping, but I was grateful Zephyr was backing me up. Sen also leaned into me, her own body a bundle of nerves. Sending calm her way too, I focused on what we needed to do. This wasn't a good situation for any of the three of us.

"Well, that may be true, but you're here to answer for your crimes. You've killed innocent—"

"No," Mr. Johnson said, cutting her off. "Aella is here to cooperate with an investigation into what happened regarding a fight between US soldiers and agents and a band of mythicals. She has been charged with no crimes, and there is no evidence that she has killed anyone. Because if there was, we all know Aella would have been arrested, not merely called in to assist with an investigation."

The woman glared at Mr. Johnson, making me feel more than a little smug. If she'd had her way, I was pretty sure he'd have dropped dead on the spot or at least been forcibly removed from the room. As it was, we needed to move on.

"Is it possible to move some of the tables so Zephyr can enter the room properly and have somewhere to sit?" I asked as if we'd not just been debating who was deadlier and whether anyone was in any danger.

Again she looked as if she might murder one of us, but eventually, she nodded.

"Yes. Have the row of tables along the back moved nearer the center to allow the dragon to spread out," she said, loudly enough that another woman in a suit jumped to attention and hurried closer. Within seconds the younger woman had men moving tables and chairs and giving Zephyr the room he needed to come inside.

Once he was through the doorway, I could see the gathering of people outside in the corridor, more than a few men and women looking in, staring at the dragon or at Sen still sitting on my shoulder.

I continued to smile and wave at anyone who looked like they might appreciate it and Sen did the same, her cuteness helping where I often failed.

More people came into our room, some of them reacting to Zephyr's presence with fear and shock when they spotted him. Others were surprised but understanding.

One more elderly woman came right up to him.

"My, my," she said. "I used to dream of something fantastical happening when I was a young girl. Of a knight of Camelot getting sent through time to sweep me off my feet, or some kind of portal opening up to a mythical world. Never thought I'd wake up one day to the news elves and dragons have been living among us for centuries."

"It blew my mind at first, too," I said.

"Of course it did," she replied, looking at me finally. "An elf. I bet that was a shock too. And now to find yourself in the position of some kind of leader or figurehead. Have you pinched yourself today?"

"No, not yet. But I've not really slept since yesterday, so I think I'm still covered by the previous one."

She laughed, taking the response the way I'd intended it.

"Well, shall we see if we can get this nasty business begun so we can rectify that?" she asked, motioning for me to follow Mr. Johnson around to a seat in front of one of the microphones.

I glanced back at Zephyr to check he was okay before going where indicated, Mr. Johnson sitting beside me. Before we could get seated and prepare, Mr. Johnson put a document he'd typed or had someone else type in front of me. I noticed there was an additional group of people on the other side of the room now, many of them with cameras and pens and paper.

It looked like the press was going to be part of this "investigation" too.

Trying not to focus on them, I looked over the document in front of me. It appeared to be a transcript of sorts of my own story, with certain sections emphasized and a few comments about better ways to say things.

I had a look through it while everyone else was seated. Sen sat herself down on the desk but kept near me. Again I tried to comfort her, but people had reacted better to her than the rest of us, and it seemed to have helped her relax a little.

"Aella-Faye, thank you for coming today," the woman from earlier said as she leaned a little closer to her mic. I noticed there was now a small plaque in front of her, bearing her name. A Mrs. Gingham.

"I don't believe I had much choice in the matter," I replied, "but you're welcome regardless. I am more than willing to come and explain my actions in a sensible manner."

I heard Mr. Johnson cough and wondered if it was a

subtle reminder I was supposed to be kind. Taking a deep breath, I reminded myself that I needed to not screw this up. It appeared that the world was watching, and I'd already gotten off to a bad start.

"Be that as it may," Mrs. Gingham said a moment later. "We'll be asking you questions about your involvement with incidents on May fifteenth this year. All questions will pertain to the day in question and the incident on that day only. Is that clear?"

"I believe so, although the incident began on the fourteenth in my understanding of it, but barely. It all started the same night and concluded on the fifteenth," I replied.

There was a flurry of paper as several people sitting at the tables opposite looked through their documents and then presented each other with sections while whispering. When Mrs. Gingham was satisfied, she looked up at me.

"Our document here states that all witness statements we have so far and the recording timestamp from the footage all indicate the incident began at approximately half-two in the morning on the fifteenth, not on the fourteenth."

"That may well be, but the incident actually began at approximately eleven that night. The altercation at the side of the road that was videoed was merely the second part of the incident."

There was another flutter of paper, clicking of pens and other rustlings.

"Please explain," Mrs. Gingham asked. "This is the first we've heard of more fighting that night."

"Yes, because the agency and soldiers involved in the second part of the fight don't want you to know that the first part involved me and several of my team rescuing a mythical they had kidnapped and tortured in an attempt to acquire the location of a hidden refuge for mythicals." I paused, hearing cameras click as the press took photos, and I was pretty sure my words were about to be heard by most of the country, if not the world.

Over the course of the next half-hour, I told the first part of my story again, focusing on the sections Mr. Johnson had suggested and repeatedly fending off Mrs. Gingham as she tried to interrupt me.

Now and then Sen looked at me, this story something she'd not been there for and only the second time she'd ever heard it. The first time I'd told it, I'd been concentrating on remembering everything, but this time I'd been over it once already. She felt a lot of different emotions, although most were sympathy for the people hurt during it.

"I repeat that I hardly see how any of this is relevant to the attack you performed on the men in question," she said for the second time, interrupting me. I held up my hand to show I wanted her to stop talking, and Mr. Johnson did the same, leaning toward his mic.

"It's my understanding that my client is allowed to answer questions as she sees fit and in her own words. She believes this to be relevant. Let her finish."

I tried not to smile as Mrs. Gingham sat back and shot him daggers with her eyes again.

"As I was saying, while rescuing the half-elf the agents and soldiers were holding captive on a nearby base, someone there informed us that we were too late to stop more of their men from attacking a particular refuge and killing every last one of the mythicals living there. Thankfully, we were quick to find their direction, and Zephyr and I flew ahead to track them down and prevent the massacre while also warning the mythicals at the refuge to prepare to defend themselves."

"And all this happened on the fourteenth?" someone else asked.

"All this happened about an hour or two before the fight at the side of the road," I explained. "The men on the road were the men on the way to massacre innocent mythicals after torturing the elf I'd rescued. So when I found the convoy, I did everything I could to slow them without them knowing I was there. I blew tires and deliberately hampered their progress. I didn't act violently toward any of the people directly until the other mythicals arrived and a fight ensued."

Finally, I stopped talking, staring at Mrs. Gingham. She had a deep frown on her face and it was clear she either hadn't been told of my words or didn't believe them. I wasn't sure which.

For the next few hours, I was invited to repeat my story, answer more questions and generally explain what I'd meant by different things, some of the people questioning me, clearly trying to trip me up and others seeming to just want to get the story straight.

I did the best I could to answer them, focusing as Mr. Johnson had recommended on believing I was preventing a massacre.

"Do you have proof?" Mrs. Gingham asked me suddenly.

"Proof of what?" I retorted, already aware of what she

was going to say but wanting it to be clear for everyone else.

"Proof that they were on their way to attack."

"I didn't record the agent who told me if that's what you're suggesting, but a group of heavily armed soldiers and men heading in the exact direction of the refuge is pretty compelling evidence all of its own, don't you think?"

"What I think is irrelevant," she snapped before someone placed a hand on her arm. She sat back and let out a frustrated sigh. I'd got under her skin, if nothing else.

"Can you prove that they were intending to attack the refuge you speak of?" someone else asked, almost apologetic about it.

"No," I replied. "Just as none of you have any proof they weren't. It's all a he-said-she-said situation in which several mythicals were killed and many more were injured while I understand that not a single agent or soldier lost their lives."

"The men and women fighting for their country getting lucky doesn't negate the intent," Gingham said. "The attack was brutal."

"Yes, it was," I said, taking a deep breath to try and calm my anger before it made me regret my words. "I stood among mythicals who had never fought a battle before in their lives as they watched their friends die for no reason other than they dared to exist in a world that doesn't want to accept them. They fought out of desperation and determination to defend what little they had left, and I think I am done here. Your minds are already made up."

I got up and looked at Zephyr, who had remained quiet

but got to his feet as well. A moment later, I picked up Sen, and she scampered up to my shoulder.

"You're done here when we say you're done," Gingham shot back, slamming her hand on the table as she also stood.

Leaning toward the microphone, I made sure my words were clear.

"You have my statement and my answers. No amount of prodding or insulting will induce me to change them. I've told you the truth. It is up to you to accept it or not. Now, I have work to get back to and mythicals to aid in finding safe places to live. If you really do think of anything else that matters to ask me, you know where I live."

"Sit back down." Gingham motioned to Mr. Johnson to stop me, but he was also on his feet, gathering up the documents he'd brought with him.

I gave Gingham my best glare and walked out anyway, Zephyr falling in beside Sen and me. I'd had enough of being put in the hot seat over something so obviously not about me getting to say my words at all. My only hope was that the press there portrayed the story honestly and accurately.

CHAPTER FIFTEEN

The stars twinkled above as Zephyr and I sat in the new roof garden we had. It was about three in the morning, and we'd not been up for very long. It had been several days since the hearing, and we'd become almost entirely nocturnal since. Although some of the public were now more sympathetic to us and what we'd been through, the government was continuing to push their agenda.

In their eyes, mythicals were uncontrolled threats with powers the American public needed to be scared of. Entities to control and study.

I shuddered as I thought about the last part and imagined labs full of mythicals being tested.

For the last few days, we'd been trying to decide what we were going to do to fight this strange battle Jacobs had tugged us into. No matter what we did, we couldn't find the man himself, and I wasn't sure what we'd do if we found him anyway.

We could abduct him and see how he likes it, Zephyr suggested.

I have a feeling that would just make the rest of the agency even more determined to kill us.

Probably. But they're already pretty determined.

Zephyr had a point, but I promised myself I wouldn't kill people unnecessarily. And I wasn't ready to let go of that ideal.

Somehow we had to find a way out of this, and we had to be better than humanity.

I was about to suggest we got some pizza, my mood still too dark to want to even joke about what we were going to do, when Minsheng appeared. He had a tray of snacks with him, and he put it down beside me.

"Thought you might like something to eat. And maybe some company. I know this isn't easy on you."

I didn't know what to say but I wasn't about to let good snacks go to waste. Sitting up, I sighed.

"I feel like it's just us against an entire world. And they don't understand that in a lot of ways I'm still just one of them."

"People like to put us in boxes and put neat little labels on them. For years I've been treated like just another Chinese chef here to try and make a fortune. But being your Shishou is my real purpose. And it breaks my heart to see you being blamed for things beyond your control."

"Great pep talk," I replied, giving Minsheng a grin to let him know I wasn't actually angry.

"I guess what I'm trying to say is you're not alone, and slowly more people are becoming accustomed to our presence. We just need a little longer and a little more belief in our innocence."

"It would help if more humans spoke up in our defense.

In that regard, we are very thin on allies."

Minsheng nodded. We slipped into a companionable silence, everyone having a munch and thinking about our future.

As Minsheng was gathering up the empty pots and putting them back on the tray, Chris appeared.

"Up for a little mission?" he asked.

"A mission?" I replied, raising my eyebrows.

"The organization called. They got a tip-off that there are some mythicals nearby who are hiding from agents trying to round them up. Another possible Shishou found them and has hidden them, but the agents are closing in. They've asked if you'll go help rescue them. Apparently, there's at least one elf among the group."

I didn't move. The organization had asked me to help. It was almost as if someone had just heard my prayers. Maybe this was a way I could get the organization to do more to help me.

Even if they don't, Zephyr said into my head, *other mythicals need us. We should go.*

Sen help. As she spoke, the myconid jumped up onto my shoulder.

It looked like we were about to go on another rescue mission. Immediately I felt a little better. Having a direct goal and people to help cleared through all the confusion.

"You're going to have to be very careful if the agency really does have a lot of heat scanners out. They'll see you coming." Minsheng frowned, clearly worried.

"I have a prototype of a little something you and Zephyr can wear," Chris replied, a light in his eyes and a smirk on his face.

"Then let's have a little test," I said, feeling better than I had in days.

Chris led us back inside the building and down to the corridor beside the kitchen and toilets that had never led anywhere. It turned out he'd begun using the space as a bit of a workshop.

"I needed to get a little help from Daisy, making sure these would fit you. But they are essentially a suit that will stop you from being detected on a heat scanner." As Chris spoke, he walked over to a stack of fabric and picked up the first small, folded bundle.

He handed it to me, the material shiny black like fake leather. There was a jacket and pants, as well as what looked like socks.

"Zephyr was a little bit harder. He's not exactly the kind of creature I can find a good pattern for. But we think we've come up with a jacket for him."

Chris picked up the final large pile of material and carried it back round to where Zephyr was waiting.

With a little bit of help from Minsheng and me, we managed to get it over him. It wasn't perfect, his head sticking out from one end and some of his tail from the other.

This feels weird, Zephyr said. *Is this what clothes feel like?*

Probably, I replied.

A moment later, I slipped into the nearby toilets and quickly got into my new outfit. It felt cold to the skin, and it didn't seem to really warm up. I had a feeling that was the point.

I'm not sure this is what clothes feel like. At least not quite like this, I told Zephyr a moment later.

"What about Sen? I asked when I was back outside again and doing up the zipper on the jacket.

"She doesn't seem to give off a heat signature the way you and Zephyr do. I don't think they'd pick her up."

"All right, I said. "Where are we going? And what am I looking out for?"

"It's a small suburb about forty-five minutes' drive from here," Chris said, pulling up a map.

Both Zephyr and I studied it. We really didn't have long to waste if the agency was already closing in.

"Let them know we're on the way if the organization has the ability to pass on the message. Get them to buy as much time as they can." I nodded to Chris and Minsheng and led my little team back to the roof.

Ready? I asked both of them.

To beat the agency? I'm always ready, Zephyr replied, a delighted light in his eyes.

Sen didn't reply but shifted to sit in the top of my jacket as she often did when we flew.

I barely had to concentrate these days to take control of the air around me and push myself up into it. After launching myself into the air, Zephyr came up beside me. Wearing our new protective outfits, we headed toward danger.

Neither of us spoke as we flew, me now settled on Zephyr's back. It felt strange to have fabric between us, but it actually made it a little easier to hold onto him.

The fabric continued to feel cold, and I was pretty sure I was beginning to shiver. This wasn't going to be a long-term solution or something we could wear all night.

As we got closer to the area we expected to find mythicals in we slowed, wanting to make sure we didn't miss signs of them.

Even if we hadn't known what house they were in or where they were hiding, Zephyr quickly spotted an agency car. We slowed and tried to make as little noise as possible as we came closer.

It took us a moment to spot the agents who went with the car. They were combing a small play park in the dark, a single flashlight between them.

Let's deal with these two before we find any more.

Use my gas, Zephyr suggested, shifting something on the inside and preparing to exhale.

I used my powers to reach for the vapor as soon as he exhaled, taking control of it and guiding it down onto the agents before they even knew we were there. Their flashlight fell to the ground sending out a beam of light onto a large bush at one end of the area.

It was a beacon of danger to any other agents nearby, and I knew we needed to turn it off.

Sen help, she said into my head as Zephyr circled. She wriggled to get out of my jacket. With one hand, I helped her, and with the other, I pushed off Zephyr's back.

See if you can find more agents and we'll come back to you, I said as I came up behind the light and helped Sen to the ground.

The small dryad scuttled over to it and quickly switched it off before running back to me with it.

Sen keep, she explained as she leaped up and onto my shoulder again, her little bouncing face smiling.

Before I could push off from the ground and go rejoin Zephyr, I heard the faint sound of a radio. I hurried over to one of the paralyzed agents and took his earpiece and a small radio.

"Ed and Harris, report your status?" a male voice said.

It took all my restraint not to respond and tell the agents that I'd taken them out. It was clear they were going to realize something had happened soon. The longer they thought it could be the mythicals already here, the better, however.

Using my abilities, I picked up both agents and quickly moved them, putting them in the back garden of a nearby house between a fence and shed as I powered back up into the air. It wasn't a perfect way to hide them, but it would make them hard to spot until they woke naturally.

Feeling a little smug, I listened as another few agents were directed to check on Ed and Harris and exercise caution.

I see them, Zephyr said a moment later. *Three agents coming this way. They've got their guns out, and they're being more careful. A flashlight each. They're not checking up, though.*

Good, I thought, lifting up a little higher and following the tug I felt toward Zephyr until I could just about see his bulky form. The large flashlights the agents carried would make us even harder to spot as long as we stayed away from street lights and houses with outside lamps.

We watched the three agents come closer, then Zephyr exhaled again, and I guided two more clouds down onto the agents.

"What the..." one of them said as it descended over his eyes, but he inhaled, and the gas' effect was swift.

He fell as the woman beside him whirled around, her gasp filling her own lungs with the same substance as the final of the three agents went down. I hadn't bothered to get on Zephyr's back so once again, I zoomed down and turned off one flashlight as Sen bounded over and turned the only other off.

Company, Zephyr said as the radio came to life again.

"Heard something to the east. We're checking it out," another agent said.

I frowned. I was standing too close to a streetlamp to be hidden by the night and not close enough to anything to get out of sight. Sen scurried over to me anyway and bounded up onto my shoulder. Not sure what else to do, I focused instead on hiding the agents from view while I jogged toward a patch of shadows behind some trees on the edge of someone's garden.

When I was still a few feet away from cover, three more agents came around a corner, guns outstretched. I blasted them off their feet with air as I sprinted behind a tree.

Bullets hit the wood and ground, sending splinters and dirt flying. The radio crackled as someone tried to speak and then I heard a yelp. I peeked out from behind the tree to see Zephyr standing over the two agents, exhaling right at their faces.

"I see the dragon," someone said into my ear.

You've been spotted, I told him. *Get into the air.*

He obeyed, a single powerful downbeat and push up from the ground enough to send him hurtling up as gun blasts broke the silence.

As dogs started to bark and a car alarm went off some-where, I wondered what the residents were going to think. We were in a suburban area full of well-kept houses and tidy gardens.

You safe? I asked Zephyr, feeling him circling back my way. A moment later I backed up so I wasn't directly under the tree and pushed up into the air as well. Flying was our advantage, and I wasn't going to neglect to use it.

"We've got the bitch and her pet in the sky," someone said into my ear, tempting me yet again to respond, even if only to tell them Zephyr wasn't a pet. I had to admit I was getting used to the agent's nickname for me.

We could get it printed on a t-shirt for you, Zephyr suggested as we flew toward each other and rejoined.

Are we going to get one that says "pet" for you too? I retorted.

Never mind.

I heard him chuckle despite the deadpan response, then we both focused, flying above the houses and trying to work out where the agents had gone.

A moment later, I spotted movement in back of a house. It could have been a basement, the house light flickering on as someone opened it a small amount.

Is that the mythicals? I asked Zephyr as we banked past and he came around to get a better look.

Looks like it might be.

We're going to need to get them out of here. They're right in the center of this estate.

Let Sen come with me and we'll cause a distraction while you get them on the move. I'm pretty sure we've opened up a hole in the agents' circle already.

Works for me, I replied, helping Sen tuck herself into the top of Zephyr's jacket before I launched up and off him.

He roared and dived toward some more agents, the fools shooting at him again with weapons that would do nothing. I hurtled toward the basement and landed right in front of it.

"I heard there were some folks here in need of a rescue," I said, but I'd already been spotted, and a face was already emerging, two hands pushing back the first of the two wooden flaps.

Grabbing the second, I pulled it back and crouched.

Down in the dim light of the basement, I made out at least six wide-eyed faces, including that of a young girl clutched in the arms of her father. This was more complicated than I'd expected.

"Come on," I said, knowing I had to act anyway. "Let's get you all somewhere safer."

They rushed up and into the open as I threw up air walls and looked for the best way out of the garden. I noticed a family of elves, a centaur, and two gnomes, but behind them came a human. A man who gave me a grateful nod. As he moved to the back gate, I got the impression that this had been his house, and he was the Shishou the organization had heard from.

I didn't doubt they all had one heck of a story to tell, but I needed to get them safe first.

Go, Zephyr said into my head as I lifted into the air. Forming a box around the mythicals, I landed ahead of them, keeping an eye on a gap, and waved them down the road to the park area we'd already cleared of agents.

I could hear more shooting and Zephyr let out another growl, no doubt trying to draw more agents to him. Fear gripped me, making me freeze. We'd never been separated in battle before. We'd always operated as a unit. I needed to know he and Sen were safe.

CHAPTER SIXTEEN

Get them out of here, Zephyr yelled into my head, unfreezing me from where I'd landed. I looked around me to see the frightened faces of the other mythicals.

They needed me, and that meant I had to focus.

"Come on, there's a clear path this way," I said.

No sooner had I spoken the words than agents rushed around the corner behind us, not noticing us at first but sprinting toward the sounds of Zephyr. As soon as they saw us, they changed direction, firing without warning.

The mythicals screamed and ran past me, but I held firm, blasting the agents with air and thickening a wall between them and us. I knocked them off their feet, temporarily halting the barrage of gunfire, and then checked the mythicals behind me. They were running blindly toward the park, the human with them clearly trying to shepherd them but struggling.

As the agents tried to get up, I hit them with another air blast and then took control of the nearest plants, reaching out vines and grabbing their guns to wrestle the weapons out of their hands.

Assaulted from both sides, the agents didn't stand a chance and were soon wrapped in plants as well. It wouldn't hold them for long, but it was enough to give us a chance to get away.

While I ran after the mythicals, keeping an eye out for danger, I reached for my burner phone and called Minsheng. He picked up after only one ring, making it obvious he was waiting up.

"What do you need?" he asked immediately.

"A ride. I've got three elves, a centaur, and two gnomes, plus the Shishou with them. They're looking terrified and tired. Also, one of them is a child."

"I'll get the bus, and we'll meet you. Keep updating your position when you can."

I hung up and tucked the phone away as I reached the group.

"Help is on the way," I said. "But we need to get you as far from the agents as we can. I'm going to need to get in the air to find the best route out of this estate and into the woods nearby. I can protect you better there."

Agents coming your way. I'm pursuing them, Zephyr said into my head as I powered upward and spotted a route out almost immediately. The Shishou led the group on, the centaur bringing up the rear as I turned to watch for signs of a threat from behind.

While I was doing this, I heard the unmistakable sound of aircraft.

Looks like we've got aerial company as well, I shot back to Zephyr, feeling him come hurtling in my direction. Just about able to make him out, I saw him pounce on some more agents and exhale.

I've dealt with about half the agents over here, but some have stuck gas masks on and another has one of those grenade launchers.

Pull back then, and we'll work together to protect this group. The Shishou seems to have recovered again and is working with me to herd them.

Just getting Sen, Zephyr replied, swooping out of sight. I saw the flash and heard the roar of the grenade launcher a moment later. Fear for my bonded mythicals stopped my heart, but a car exploded, and even more alarms went off.

Lights started to flick on up and down the streets. It was definitely time to get out of here.

After guiding the refugees even farther out of the estate, I hung back from the group for now as Zephyr came flying toward me with Sen, unharmed but looking serious.

I could hear a stream of commands through my earpiece but I couldn't understand all of them, the orders in code, almost as if they suspected that I was listening in.

Trying to concentrate, I let Zephyr take on the job of leading the group, the dragon flying lower so he could be seen and Sen using the flashlight she'd stolen to occasionally pinpoint the path for the mythical refugees.

I kept a wall up around them, but flying for so long and the constant use of my abilities was starting to tire me. Not to mention that I still felt so cold I was shivering.

More than once while we fled—the agents hanging back for now—I considered ripping the jacket off, pretty sure I'd feel warmer if I *wasn't* wearing it. There was no way I was letting the agents get their hands on a prototype, however.

I didn't want them to know what we were working on. It was bad enough that they'd have seen Zephyr in his strange coat. Hopefully, they'd just think it was armor we'd had him wear after the last attack.

The mythicals we were escorting just made it to the edge of the forest when more agency cars came roaring up, agents and soldiers pouring out, already wearing gas masks. Three fighter jets came roaring overhead.

One of the mythicals screamed, although the Shishou tried to calm them and encourage them farther into the trees.

Sen, go with them and guide them south, I said into her head.

Sen lead, she replied, leaping from Zephyr's back to a tree and then down onto the Shishou.

"Sen," she said, pointing at herself. "Come."

Then she bounded off using the flashlight to guide them.

I immediately felt the tug of her moving farther from me, but Zephyr and I had work to do.

You take the agents on the ground, and I'll take care of the planes? Zephyr suggested as the fighter jets banked back around.

Exhale on the agents first, I replied. *Make it hard for them to see if nothing else.*

I'd barely finished speaking before Zephyr was doing it, sweeping over them and ignoring the bullets they fired to cover them in vapor. Instantly I took control of it and pulled it in as densely over them as I could.

"Dragon seems to be masking his heat signature," someone said on the radio channel. "We just got gassed from nowhere."

"No sign of the bitch either."

I grinned, grateful the clothes were working even if they were freezing me. It gave me an advantage. The planes came back around, aiming for the mythicals behind us and forcing Zephyr and I to both pull back and deal with them.

They opened fire, shooting into the trees, but Zephyr soon flew in the way, taking the hits to protect the others, his scales deflecting the bullets with very little in the way of pain. I threw up another air barrier between them anyway and then powered myself after the nearest jet. Getting close to the plane, I tried to look for some way I could disable it.

Any idea where the fuel is on these things? I asked, but I knew it was pointless. Zephyr pulled up in front of one of the other jets, and the pilot opened fire. Seeing where the bullets were coming from, I blasted that section of the plane with as much air pressure as I could muster quickly. Something inside it exploded, rocking the jet and stopping it from firing.

Zephyr literally landed on one of the others, weighing it down and tearing at the outside with his claws.

The pilot ejected as Zephyr pulled away, taking something important with him. I had to slow the wreckage and help it crash-land into the surface of a road. It made a huge mess, but it was better than it killing anyone or breaking something valuable.

That left one jet, but for now, it was heading in the wrong direction again.

I'll deal with it. You protect the group again, Zephyr said, flying after the only undamaged jet.

Again, I had to push down my fear and focus on our task. Reaching for my connection to Sen, I worked out where the mythicals had got to. They weren't moving very fast, Sen having taken them off the main path, but I trusted her to guide them through well enough; after all, she was in her natural habitat, and the trees pretty much answered to her.

Landing to rest, I put myself between the group and the agents and waited in the dark, listening and watching.

Although Zephyr's vapor hadn't knocked any of them out, I knew his gas was growing more potent, and it could be absorbed by the skin. With any luck, it would have made the agents coming my way more sluggish.

Now and then my earpiece came to life, agents checking in with their commander and reporting no sign of me and nothing on the heat sensors. I grinned as I heard them coming closer.

They were in the forest now, and with my recent ability to control earth and trees, they'd walked right into an entire arsenal. Taking several deep breaths to calm down, I concentrated and reached into the trees ahead of me, feeling for the agents within their branches and roots.

It was a strange sensation, as if I had sensors and limbs all over the place. With those limbs, I reached out and latched onto weapons, diving with branches and moving the earth to make pits and boulders where there hadn't been any before.

Wildlife shifted in the tumultuous movement, making me feel a little guilty that I was wrecking their homes and upsetting their habitat, but I did my best to avoid anything I could sense out there.

The agents shouted and screamed as I yanked them off their feet, caught them in holes they couldn't climb out of alone, or stole their weapons and held them out of their reach.

Although I found taking control of the earthen elements almost as easy as I did the air, I wasn't as practiced and it didn't take long for me to feel exhausted, a dull ache beginning to form in my head.

Thankfully, the few agents I'd not managed to stop backed up to the edge of the forest and did their best to take their comrades with them.

I let them go, more worried about the mythicals we were rescuing and Zephyr dealing with the final jet.

You okay? I asked him as I took off jogging after Sen, trying not to trip over a root or smack into a branch in the dark forest.

A few bruises on my body and holes in this strange outfit Chris has made, but otherwise fine. Nice work bringing the forest to life.

I grinned as I reached out to feel the world around me with my abilities. It helped me move a little quicker, my mind sensing the trees and bushes around me before I could see them with my eyes.

It didn't take me long to catch up with Sen and the refugees. They'd stopped for a break, the female elf and one of the gnomes sitting down while the others stood and waited.

"We have a vehicle coming to collect us all," I said by way of an introduction. "But I think we're going to need to keep moving. The agency won't let us keep going without pursuing us, I'm sure."

"Thank you for all you do," the other Shishou said. "I didn't know what to do or where to turn. We had been training and living happily as a small community until three days ago."

"It's okay," I said. "We'll find you all somewhere safe again, I promise. No one is going to harm any of you while Zephyr, Sen, and I are here. And more of my friends are on the way to help."

The woman on the floor reached her hand up and took mine to give it a squeeze.

"You bring great hope to our kind, Henera. May you always be blessed."

I lifted my eyebrows, not sure what she had meant by the name she'd given me, but as I heard noises coming from behind us and thought I could detect more aircraft, it was clearly not time to discuss it.

"We need to get moving again," I said, slightly worried that I wasn't going to be able to completely fulfill my promise. I was exhausted already and had been using my powers constantly for some time now.

The Shishou nodded and encouraged the to keep moving, acting like the leader they needed. It helped me feel calmer to see them all working together and moving on. We just needed to lose the agents on our tail.

I updated Minsheng on our location with a quick text as we moved more southwest and aimed for the western edge of the forest we were in. We'd need to find a road or track soon or he wasn't going to be able to pick us up, but equally, we didn't want to get there too soon or we'd find the agents holding us up and stopping us from getting away.

As we continued, however, it was clear that the agents weren't interested in doing anything but following us for now, a helicopter flying overhead and agents moving through the trees.

While they kept their distance, I didn't use my powers, but I was starting to get worried.

I think they're up to something, I told Zephyr. *Can you fly ahead and see what it might be?*

Already thinking the same thing. Heading forward.

As Zephyr increased the distance between us again, I tried not to let the strange feeling steal my focus. It was imperative I kept an eye out and protected everyone.

Several times I looked back, traveling at the back of the group while Sen continued to lead, but the agents kept out of sight, and even when I felt for them with the branches of trees and vines from plants they were spread out and scattered, like they were forming a long barrier behind us. Like we were being herded toward something.

They've got cars on the road ahead. And more agents. All wearing masks. Couple of grenade launchers and other heavy-duty weapons too. Pretty sure there's also a tank. No. Wait. Make that two, Zephyr said into my head a moment later.

Shitsticks. That was a lot of firepower. There was no way we could walk into that. But it also presented another big question. How did they know we were coming their way?

The heat signatures, Zephyr suggested. *You and me are protected and clearly not being detected, but the others are giving off plenty of heat.*

I frowned. Zephyr had a point, but we needed them not to be detectable if we were going to all get out of this alive. They needed to get out of the area and off in another direction.

As the elven woman and the gnome both begged for another rest, I let them stop.

"Just two minutes and then we need to get moving again. They're still not giving up." I nodded at the Shishou to hopefully make it clear that I expected him to be the one to reinforce my time limit.

It bought me a little more time to think of a good plan. We needed to mask all their heat signatures and get them past the agents and out of this trap we were being pushed toward.

Zephyr, I need you to land, I projected his way. *We need your large heatproof cloak.*

There's a clearing just to your left. Should be big enough, he replied as he darted down toward it. He landed with a thump that I helped muffle and keep contained.

I motioned for the group to head over to him as I jogged closer. As soon as I reached him, I began undoing the straps that held it in place.

Going to need you to be a distraction once more. Think you can do that? I asked.

If it means I get to wreck another tank, I'm all for it. Those things are annoying.

Only if it won't kill anyone and you're careful not to let your defenses down. You don't need to stop any of them. Just distract them for long enough. As I spoke, I ushered the group of refugees under the blanket-like mass of fabric and ejected Zephyr out the other side.

It was a quick and dirty hack, but I then had the group huddle together under the cloak, draping it around them as best I could and using my powers to hold it in place while circulating the air underneath for them.

Sen, lead them back the way we've come. I'll make you a gap and help Zephyr distract everyone.

Sen keep safe, she replied, sounding almost happy about having such an important task. I smiled at her enthusiasm and moved the trees to make them subtly denser around the route the mythicals were taking, guiding the agents to either side around them.

I went with them, a few yards behind, and Zephyr stayed where he was.

"Looks like they're pausing up ahead," the agent in charge said in my earpiece, confusing Zephyr for the mythicals.

I tried not to panic and worry about my dragon as the mythicals continued to sneak away. I kept an eye on the agents on either side. It was important no one detected them or realized they'd doubled back.

Into the air, Zephyr, I said. *And fly low, like you're burdened.*

He chuckled in my head as I boosted the updraft under his wings to help him get into the air better. As he did, I noticed he grabbed a large fallen tree and made it look like he was carrying something. I reached for it and tried to infuse it with heat, pushing hot air into it and trying to make the tree produce some as well.

Although I had no idea if it was working, the agents picked up on his sudden movement.

"I think they're on the dragon and trying to fly south,"

the agent said. "I repeat. It appears that they have loaded onto the dragon and are flying south."

"Roger that. I have him on the scanner as well. Appears to be carrying something, possibly their belongings or an injured mythical and is flying low. I'm in pursuit."

I took a deep breath to calm myself, wanting to rush to Zephyr's defense, but the mythicals still weren't clear enough of the danger for me to feel like I could leave them just yet.

The stretch between our bonds and the distance between us was also starting to have an impact. My stomach felt as if it was being pulled in two separate directions. I did what I needed, however, using my cell to update Minsheng once again and let him know what to look out for.

When I could wait no longer, I decided to cause more havoc and flew toward the small arsenal of weaponry and soldiers by the road. If they were just going to sit there, I was going to see what I could sabotage on the sly.

CHAPTER SEVENTEEN

I didn't fly. Instead, I snuck through the forest in a more westerly direction, hoping I was going straight enough. Having Sen and Zephyr in different directions helped me think of us as three points of a triangle that was growing.

Be careful, Zephyr said as he flew farther away, his voice a little quieter. *They're looking for you.*

I could say the same to both you and Sen, I replied. *We don't have much choice. We need them confused and without much to fight.*

We do, but we also need to stay alive and unhurt.

Noted.

I frowned as I slowed, seeing lights ahead and not wanting to get too much closer. If I was going to cause any damage, I needed to do it carefully and slyly.

Hunkering down, I watched and waited. I could see one of the men with a grenade launcher clearly trying to track something in the sky.

Worried that it was Zephyr, I reached out with the

vines from a nearby tree, and with a flick, wrapped the vine around the gun and pulled it out of his grasp.

There were shouts and yells, and I saw agents running this way.

I ducked down behind a large tree as they shone flashlights into the forest. As I did, I reached out for more of the forest and took control of all the trees along the edge of the road. Immediately I could sense where most of the agents were as they came into the forest. I shot more vines and branches out, knocking the agents back or stringing them up where they could do no harm. Along the way, I broke as many of the flashlights as I could.

It was chaos, but I quickly grew tired and felt my powers waning again. As much as this was useful, I couldn't keep it up much longer.

Stopping, I listened and felt with the trees. The agents had pulled back and were on their guard, guns pointed at the trees and gas masks on. If I was going to break the tank a little farther up the road, I needed to get on with it.

Moving closer and heading from tree to tree, I tried to get an accurate idea of where it was. I wanted to disable the gun and the tracks if I could. But I was also going to have to make sure I didn't hurt anyone. Given everything that was going on, I was pretty sure even a slight injury was going to make some people feel vindicated in their opinion of me.

Eventually, I could just about see the tank and still be mostly hidden from view. I stopped and reached into the forest again. This time I also connected with the trees on the other side of the track. It was already beginning to make my head hurt, but I managed to slowly reach vines across the ground and sneak them up the side of the tank, wrapping them around the gun and tracks.

I paused there, feeling light-headed.

Aella? Zephyr's voice came into my head, sounding farther away than it ought to. *Are you safe? You feel...strange. Like you're not as connected.*

I'm okay, I replied, not giving any more details. I felt a similar strain to the connection too.

I'm coming back your way. Is Minsheng there yet?

Sen waiting, she shot back, answering Zephyr's question for me. I didn't respond, knowing I had to move fast if I didn't want the soldiers and agents to notice the vines I'd moved into position.

After taking a couple of deep breaths and letting my vision clear more, I reached out again and quickly wrapped the vines around the gun. Squeezing, I tried to bend it downwards. I wrapped more vines around the tracks on one side, away from most of the other agents.

Again I heard shouts and dismayed cries, but I ignored them as best I could and focused on the task.

The gun eventually popped and twisted, but something flared in my head, making me wince.

As my head throbbed, I had no choice but to let go of the rest of the forest. I tried to move, but my limbs wouldn't respond properly. In the background, I could hear the agents trying to rush around again, and lights flickered here and there, people trying to find me on both sides of the road, not buying my attempt to draw their attention elsewhere.

Might need some help, I said, trying to reach for Zephyr. *I overcooked it.*

There was no response. I wasn't connected to Sen and Zephyr anymore. I couldn't feel either of them.

"She's got to be around here somewhere," a voice yelled in my ear, responding to the radio chatter between the agents. It helped focus me a little, but I still felt as if all my limbs were lead weights, each one shaking and achy.

I'd way overcooked it.

Taking several deep breaths, I tried not to panic. The agents didn't know where I was, and for now, I was still hidden in the dark. I had time to rest a moment and see if I could quickly recover.

I'd only been sitting there for a minute or so, lights flickering across the forest around me as agents started heading my way to look. Now the trees were still and no longer under my control, they'd gained confidence. A moment later, my cell buzzed.

I quickly pulled it out and checked my messages.

I've got to Sen and the mythicals. All in the bus, but Sen is going nuts, doesn't want to leave and keeps jabbering about you being lost. Please tell me you're okay.

Taking a few more deep breaths and starting to feel steady, I tapped out a quick response.

Not lost. Tell Sen I'll be back in a few minutes. Just pushed a little hard and I'm not currently in good range to feel Sen. Take them all home, Zephyr, and I will catch up.

It wasn't exactly the whole truth, but it was enough to

stop both of them worrying, and it meant I only had to find Zephyr.

As I got shakily to my feet, my head stayed clear. I was still hidden behind a tree, but I could hear the agents coming closer, the lights they were projecting shaking and growing more focused and specific as they approached my position.

If I didn't move soon, I was going to have to contend with the agents. But I needed to get past their lights. It wasn't going to be easy.

Thankfully, some animal chose that moment to dart near an agent and several of the lights flicked over to where it had been. I sprinted off into the darkness they left behind, aware I was catching leaves and branches as well. I could only hope I was quieter than the noise the agents made and the animals they were disturbing.

I still couldn't feel Zephyr, but I kept running anyway, heading for whichever part of the forest seemed darkest. As I did, I occasionally ducked behind a tree to get my breath back and rummage for some food in my pockets and a small bag.

After getting the message to come rescue the mythicals, I'd left in such a hurry that I'd forgotten to take anything with me. I was going to have to rely on my abilities regenerating the slow way: with time and rest.

I'd been running for several minutes when I opted to slow and try to reach for Zephyr again. He'd been heading toward the agents behind me so I didn't want to get too far away and not be able to easily tell him where I was.

No sooner had I stopped than the agents came back into view, more flashlights appearing behind me. I still couldn't feel Zephyr, and worry about his safety made my stomach knot in painful waves. What if something had happened to him in the meantime?

Taking a deep breath and trying to ignore my fear, I carried on, turning a little to the left to try and head back north and toward where Sen had been heading. With any luck, Zephyr would fly back in that direction if he got to the agents and still couldn't feel me.

I walked more slowly, having to pick my way through the forest with nothing but a partial moon to light my way. With the agents behind me far enough, they didn't interfere with my lighting, my eyes had adjusted, but it was still dark.

Periodically I tried to reach for Zephyr again, but there was still nothing. As each minute went by, the fear grew until it was consuming all my thoughts. Where was he, and why couldn't I feel him?

I was almost back at the edge of the forest when I felt the air blowing around me and my connection to it returned, my body naturally forming a small shield around myself as I'd been doing every waking moment for months. That made me feel a little calmer. I wasn't entirely defenseless anymore.

Trying to decide what to do next, I felt the tension grow in my stomach until I realized it wasn't fear and doubt but the usual unraveled feel of my insides at Zephyr being a long way off.

There you are, his voice said into my head a moment later, as full of relief as I was. *I lost you.*

I know, I replied, stopping short of telling him that I'd done too much. I felt as if I should have known better.

Where's Sen? I still can't feel her.

Too far away, I think. Or my connection to that element hasn't returned yet.

I could feel Zephyr flying closer, the strange sensation in the pit of my stomach lessening and giving me some relief. For now, I waited for him, safely in the shadows of the forest. I didn't have the energy to fly up to him, but he was speeding toward me, and the gap was closing faster than I thought any agents had time to breach.

As Zephyr came closer, I felt better, and slowly I reached out and connected with more around me until I was once again able to control things in my usual way. It was only then that I noticed the bundle of fabric at the edge of the forest. I walked toward it, finding Zephyr's heatproof jacket. There were a few holes in it now and tears, but it would help us get away.

My body was still being slowly made colder by the jacket I wore, although the discomfort seemed to have lessened a little. Again I considered taking it off, but at the last moment, I decided not to. It hopefully wouldn't be much longer before we were back at the warehouse and safe once more.

When Zephyr got really close, I came out of the forest so he could land beside me.

I'd refuse to wear this thing if we didn't know it worked, Zephyr said into my head as he touched down beside me. *It's probably saved those mythicals' lives, hasn't it?*

I think so. It allowed them to sneak past the agents in the dark. That's better than nothing.

Better let Chris know he got something right then, Zephyr

acknowledged as I quickly fitted it back onto him, tying it up as best I could.

By the time I was done, I felt exhausted again. I really wished I'd brought some food with me.

We could get something on the way back.

It's not far. If you can manage, let's just get home. It will probably be almost dawn. We can see if Holfin will cook us his enormous breakfast.

Deal. Hop on. You're out of magic juice, aren't you?

I paused as Zephyr turned his head to me and looked me right in the eyes.

I'm no fool, Aella. There are only two ways the connection between us is blocked or severed. One of us dies, or the magic isn't strong enough to combat something in the way, like distance. You pushed yourself too far and couldn't reach across the distance anymore.

Sighing, I nodded. He was right, and I felt like I'd let him down.

Come on. Let's go home before the agents find us again.

Needing no other reminder that we weren't safe yet, I climbed up and settled in my usual position on Zephyr's back. Without my help, it took him a slight run-up and push-off before he got into the air and above the trees, but he was soon powering us home.

I held on, feeling even colder as I barely had the energy to keep the wind off me. Instead, I hunkered lower on his back, pressing myself as flat as I could and keeping my head down behind Zephyr's.

We flew in almost silence, tiredness overwhelming me and giving me no energy for anything but holding on. At some point we passed close to the agents on the road, but

Zephyr didn't stop and give them a chance to spot us. They were no longer a threat to anyone tonight, most of them strung up in trees or trying to get their tank moving again.

Almost there, Zephyr said as we started to fly over the LA suburbs. It wasn't long after that I felt the first inkling that Sen was nearby, a thread seeming to unravel from somewhere deep inside me and reach out to the city below.

Sen, are you all right? I asked, hoping she could hear me finally.

I heard her squeal and felt the warmth, relief, and delight at being connected again to her emotions and mine.

Sen safe. Others safe. With Shishou, she replied, saying more than she ever had. I marveled at the growing communication between us and took some comfort from it.

Zephyr slowed as we came in over the warehouse and landed. I could feel Sen even more clearly now, her little body somewhere in the building below. Coming back toward her was a relief in so many ways, and it immediately helped me feel better.

Before we could get all the way down to the kitchen, she came bounding up the stairs and into my arms, nuzzling into my jacket and settling there as if she didn't plan to move ever again.

Instantly I felt better, calmer in a way I couldn't describe. She was safe and we were all together again.

We paused, the three of us just there together, before we continued to the kitchen. We were partway down the final set of stairs when I noticed that there was a commotion by the front door. Crawley sat on the floor in front of someone else, Minsheng and Chris both supporting whoever was lying down.

"What's happened?" I asked as I rushed forward.

"Emily was attacked," Daisy said as she rushed over out of the kitchen, the first aid kit in her hands.

As I got closer, I saw that Chris was bleeding; he had a cut over his eyebrow and two more on his arms. There was also a bruise on his jaw, a taser was sticking out of his jeans, and a dart gun was lying discarded on the floor near Crawley.

Emily was in the worst shape, however. Her arm was broken and her eye was swollen shut.

"How? When?"

"While you were all gone," Crawley said, her voice strained as if she was struggling to hold herself together. I looked between the mother and daughter and knew there was more than a little reason to be. The whole time I'd known her, Crawley had just wanted to protect her daughter, and now both of them had been dragged into a massive fight neither truly wanted a part of.

Unable to do much to help, I simply sat on the floor with them and tried not to get in the way. Something had to change. Mythicals were being hurt and attacked all over the place, and no one believed me.

As Daisy agreed to take Emily to the hospital and the organization confirmed they'd foot the bill, I made my way to the kitchen with Zephyr and Sen.

We'll find a way to stop this happening, Zephyr said into my head as I mechanically grabbed frozen pizzas and stuck them in the oven.

How? I demanded, turning around and almost hurling

the pizza box I'd just picked up. *How are we ever going to make them trust us when the very way we look seems to fill them with fear?*

I don't know yet, he replied, coming to stand close again, his eyes right in front of mine, his expression firm and confident.

All the energy and aggression left me and I leaned forward, resting my head against his.

We can't give up, he said. *They need us to find a way through. They need us to lead the mythicals into a better existence.*

I don't know if we can.

We can. One day at a time.

CHAPTER EIGHTEEN

As Daisy took the plates off the table and went to put them in the dishwasher, I found I didn't want to move.

"Thank you, Holfin," I said instead, having just finished the epic breakfast he'd already become famous for.

"Don't mention it. I think we all needed it." He patted my shoulder before heading out of the room, his words more than a little heartfelt. He'd been one of the first people I'd rescued with Zephyr once our nature had been known to the world. It wasn't hard for him to understand what everyone else was going through.

I felt very mixed. We'd all slept a little and Daisy and Emily had returned from the hospital in the morning, Emily wearing a cast and sling. She was now resting in one of the small rooms on the top floor.

If I'd been in the warehouse or nearby, I could have got to her. Instead, Chris, Crawley and Daisy had gone to her rescue, the three of them outnumbered and without any powers.

Of course, Crawley and Daisy had enough training and

experience to prevail, but it had been close. And I couldn't stop thinking about how much it sucked that I hadn't been there because I'd been somewhere else saving other mythicals from a similar fate.

I was still sitting at the table when Crawley came in and sat down.

"I'm going to go to the press," she said. "Like you asked. I'm going to tell them everything."

Blinking, I didn't know how to respond at first.

"Do you want me to come with you? I asked a moment later. She shook her head.

"It's better if I go alone. The more I seem to have chosen this without your interference the better. I want to be believed. Emily needs me to do this for her sake. You've made it so different now, my strategy of being good and toeing the line to keep her out of danger won't work anymore. I need to start helping you fight for a world she can live safely in."

"Thank you," I said. "I know you're doing it for her and not for me, but I think you're doing the right thing. You have a powerful voice in this."

"And it's time I used it." With a nod my way, Crawley walked out of the room and toward the front door.

Finally, something that will make a difference, Zephyr said into my head. *Maybe everything that has happened so far is for the best. It is awful that Emily was hurt, but having people realize you won't be able to protect everyone if they don't start fighting for what's right themselves is good for everyone.*

It is. Let us hope it actually helps, however, I said as I got to my feet.

Want to train while we wait to find out? Zephyr asked.

If we have time. Minsheng asked us to escort the new mythicals to the Sanctuary. The family of elves and the centaur are keen to get there as soon as they can, and Minsheng is going to have to drive them most of the way. They can't walk all that way with one of them injured and the young elf still in shock.

Getting up, we made our way to the dojo area of the building, finding Minsheng, Erlan and the new Shishou all sitting together around a flaming ball that was hovering in the air and moving in a very controlled fashion.

"Nice," I said, knowing that Erlan had been struggling with such precision in his control. He briefly looked my way and grinned.

"Jinto here helped me," he said. "He always hoped for a fire elf to teach, so he knows a lot more about our specific skills."

"Cool." I sat down, giving Erlan both the space and the attention for now. He spent the next few minutes showing me what he was now capable of, also holding flames in several locations at once.

It was impressive progress.

"I must confess, I had no idea you were so much more impressive than the average elf," Jinto said to me once Erlan was done and his flame winked out. "Everything you did to aid us last night was phenomenal. And if I understand it correctly, you have mastered two elements."

"I'd say I've only truly mastered one, but I'm learning with the other. It's a work in progress."

"Which one came first?"

"Air. Then Earth. I have the water master at the Sanctuary trying to get me to master that one next."

Jinto nodded, his eyes going wide.

"What?" I asked when he looked at Minsheng and patted the man on the shoulder.

"I've known Minsheng for a while. We joined the organization at the same time, and they have made no secret that they exist not just for elves but with the hope of finding an elf who can control more than one element. Most of us didn't believe it possible. All the elves we trained had only ever had one affinity. And of course, we've always been in hiding."

"The organization weren't exactly forthcoming with the reason why they thought an elf with multiple powers would appear," Minsheng replied, sounding as if he was trying to make Jinto feel better.

"No, but you believed it anyway. You held onto that hope and even dared to hope you might be that Shishou..." Jinto looked between us again. "You're one lucky bastard."

Minsheng only grinned.

"Would you do me the honor of showing me what else you're capable of? he asked.

"Well, it's a moving bar at the moment. We're still working Sen into the possibilities, but I'm sure we can show you some of the stuff we're capable of," I said as I got up again, making sure it was clear that we were a team. Once again, someone had assumed it was all down to me.

Quickly the three of us launched into a routine, starting with the skills we'd been training, my abilities complementing the skills of the two bonded mythicals.

I focused on what we could do together and using my powers to help them and then to enhance something I was trying to do. We even made our way through the agent

196

assault course we'd designed, showing Jinto how quickly we could tackle all of the targets.

"That's amazing," he said when we were standing on the finish line, all three of us panting but grinning. We'd managed to shave off about twelve seconds from our best time in that setup, and it always felt good to push ourselves in a safer setting.

"I also understand that you're capable of creating tornadoes," Jinto said when we didn't immediately move to attempt anything else. "My books have illustrations of Tuviel doing the same thing in a large battle once. Is it truly possible?"

I nodded, but I didn't begin attempting to show it to him. There wasn't the space in the warehouse for me to start something that destructive and let it build without running the risk of breaking something. And Lyra's little dojo business was struggling enough thanks to me. She didn't need me making it any worse on her.

"Maybe we should take a break, have some food, and see how Crawley is doing," Minsheng suggested, his eyes flicking to Jinto a couple of times. I was pretty sure there was a hint of concern in his voice, but I wasn't sure why. I did know I trusted Minsheng, however. If he thought we should stop for some reason, I was going to do exactly that.

Jinto seems very keen to see everything we can do. Minsheng probably just wants us to be careful not to let the public know exactly what we're capable of, Zephyr suggested. *It's better for us if the world continues to underestimate us.*

But Jinto is another Shishou, I thought, projecting the words to Zephyr as we climbed up the stairs and made our way to the kitchen.

Yes, but if Minsheng doesn't entirely trust him, perhaps there is a good reason.

I exhaled, not sure how to respond or what to think. I didn't want to worry that someone in the warehouse wasn't entirely on our side. Everyone else had known we were allies. Even Crawley had started helping us.

We were soon eating. Holfin and Justin had cooked a dish together that Minsheng's aunt had taught them. It was heavenly and soon made me feel stronger again. I expected to be asked to show off my skills once more, but Minsheng appeared to deliberately steer Jinto into agreeing to talk to the organization about the future of the Shishous.

Left alone in the kitchen, I considered flying out into the night, but I suspected after the action of the previous night that we'd need the heatproof clothing if we wanted solitude. And we weren't exactly in Chris' good graces.

We'd informed him of our troubles with the fabric. How it made us feel really cold although it had been very useful. It didn't help that Zephyr's suit had come back full of holes. Chris wasn't the happiest right now.

On top of that, he was licking his wounds. He had some serious bruises from taking a few punches and kicks meant for Emily.

I frowned and stood from the table, but we didn't get very far before Emily herself appeared. She smiled at me despite the bruises on her face and I immediately got her a plate of dinner and cut it up so she could eat it with her good hand.

"Thank you," she said a moment later, taking the first bite and letting out an appreciative noise. "I really needed this."

"How are you doing?"

"I still hurt a little, but less so. I have been assured that most of the bruises will actually feel worse tomorrow and the day after, however.

"I'm so sorry that I wasn't there to help you," I said, every mark on her a reminder I had failed to protect someone I'd promised I would.

"Actually, I think it might have been a good thing in some ways."

Called it, Zephyr said into my head. I shot him a look as Emily looked away, focusing on her food.

Not sure what else to do, I sat down again and waited for her to explain what she thought was the silver lining to the cloud.

"I think I'm actually a water elf," she said. "The drinks I'd been carrying sort of...came to my defense partway through the fight. They shook themselves up and the lids popped off like little bullets from a gun, hitting the attackers and pushing them back. It didn't last, and they were more pissed at me than ever, but I'm pretty sure I did it."

"The water master at the Sanctuary mentioned that an affinity can come out in elves when they are in highly stressful situations," I replied. "Ruehnar keeps trying to get me to try and use water when I need to, but I don't know how to do it."

"Can I come with you when you go to the Sanctuary next? I would like to learn more, and as much as I'm sure Minsheng would be lovely and is trying to help, I think this one feels...different than the others. He's spoken of how you reach out and connect to the air and earth."

"Yes, it's as if they open up to me and my connection."

"I think water is different. There's so much living in it. It gets in the way, makes it hard to focus on the water. But last night I...became the water and the soda. It was..." Her voice trailed off, but I nodded encouragingly.

"Strange," I finished for her a moment later.

"Everything about this feels strange. I mean, I didn't even know I was an elf until I found my mother's memory box of my father. She'd raised me to be human, and I looked mostly human." Emily looked away, almost crying, but she took several deep breaths and somehow held herself together.

I reached out and placed my hand gently on hers.

"You've got plenty of time to work out who you are and who you want to be. And I'll definitely take you to the Sanctuary. You can stay there as long as you want."

"Thank you," she replied, turning her eyes up to me and smiling through the emotion. "Mother was right in saving you and letting you grow. You're going to be amazing at leading our kind into a better future."

While I appreciated the vote of confidence, I was also slightly nervous about being put on such a high pedestal. It made it clear what I needed to do next, however. I needed to take a bunch of people to the Sanctuary, and we had to hope that Crawley's words were going to help sway the US government and the citizens of this country so they began to believe we weren't a threat.

Needing something to focus on until we had to leave, I made my way to the dojo again and pulled out a bow. It wasn't something I needed to learn to do, but it used all my abilities, and it helped me calm down. It also gave Sen and

Zephyr free space and time to do as they pleased. We might have been bonded, but we were still three separate entities with different desires and needs.

I was still doing that when Ronan appeared, automatically giving me a few small pointers to help me get even more accurate and rely on my abilities less to hit the target spot on.

"You're bothered," Ronan said when I had scored all over the target.

"Yes. I'm worried about Crawley and Emily, Crawley especially. She's sticking her neck out to help us, and the more I see of the humans, the more I'm sure they want to just see us behind bars. They think we're subverting justice," I blurted out, not entirely sure where my thoughts had come from despite the truth of them. Maybe I'd needed a moment to stop and actually process.

"They have a fixed idea of justice, and in some ways, they have a good point. There should always be accountability. It is why the Sanctuary has a council with members of most of the races on it. It allows them to feel represented and protected."

"But we've promised that we'd hold the mythicals to account. That we'd police them ourselves. I've offered it many times." I was pouting and getting grumpy, but I couldn't help it.

"In some ways, yes. They can see you standing in charge of the other mythicals. But who holds you to account? No one appears to. You keep telling them what you think and who you think you are, but no one they trust has checked your life. That's what this investigation is all about." Ronan gave me yet more arrows and stood back to give me room to shoot them."

"But I'm cooperating with their investigation. And I've told them everything."

"You have, but not until summoned, and even then, you were reluctant to do so. It has been spun to make it appear that you believe yourself above it, has it not? That you don't have to answer to the same rules. You keep claiming that we're no different and want to be like any other American citizen, but we're not letting them hold us to account like they do other citizens."

As Ronan finished speaking, I shot the arrows into the target in rapid succession, getting off a set of better shots this time. I had a feeling that Ronan had a point, even if I didn't like it, but I had no idea what to do about it.

At least, not yet.

CHAPTER NINETEEN

As the Sanctuary came into view, I felt myself relax. We'd been flying above the bus for over an hour, and then when the road had turned into a track that didn't accommodate any more progress, we'd come to a halt, and everyone had piled out.

Since then, Zephyr had been carrying Emily, and I'd been helping the elven family and their little girl hobble along toward the Sanctuary. It didn't help that it was situated partway up the mountain.

Before we were even at the border, I saw a couple of the guards come out of the small lookout post and hop down to greet us.

"Ronan said to expect visitors again," the nearest dwarf said. "Welcome, welcome. We have warm beds waiting for all of you and some food and drink should you need sustenance. Does anyone require medical aid?"

"Beds and food and drink should suffice," I said as I landed not too far from him. "Any injuries we bear were received before this night. We have traveled in peace this evening."

The dwarf looked relieved but not too pleased to see me. I tried to give him a smile, but it came out a little forced. Zephyr also landed, and Emily almost toppled from his back.

I used my powers to stop her hurting herself further. Slowly, I set her down on her feet, and then Crawley came up behind her.

"You have a human with you?" the dwarf asked as she stared at the city before her.

"Yes, Emily's mother. She's human but has every desire to see us safe, along with her daughter," I shot back, not sure I liked the attitude the dwarf had shown. I'd personally assured Crawley that she'd be welcome to come with us, especially after standing up for us in the public investigation.

It had been hard to read people's reactions to her, and there was talk of Crawley being arrested for admitting that she hadn't followed orders. Of course, those orders had been to kill me for doing nothing more than finding an egg and protecting it while it hatched. She'd been sure to make that point.

"Aella and friends," Lorcan said a moment later, the centaur stepping out of the shadows. "Come this way. I will guide you to your beds."

I smiled and bowed to the centaur, the first member of the Sanctuary council to overtly accept me and my presence in the city as a good thing.

We all moved deeper and I let the others head after Lorcan, keeping to the back with Minsheng, Sen, and

Zephyr. The whole city was quiet, other than the guards and the few mythicals who preferred the nighttime, and I didn't intend to wake anyone.

Although I felt more welcome here than I had in a long time, I wasn't going to be rocking boats if I could help it.

Lorcan led us to a large building that had been designed with Zephyr in mind. We'd slept there a few times already, and I was grateful to find the room we'd used exactly as we'd left it, almost as if someone had officially allocated it to us so we could drop in any time. Of course, it made sense, given Zephyr was the only dragon, that the room designed for him would always be kept aside for us.

Everyone else was quick to get into their own ornate and beautiful rooms made from a mix of plant life and stone, except for Minsheng, Zephyr, Sen, and me.

We settled down around a small fire, deciding to eat before resting after such a long journey.

The large pot of stew simmering near the fire had filled the central living area of the building with a heavenly smell. Lorcan joined us, and I handed him a bowl.

"Tell me how all of you have been doing these last few weeks," I asked Lorcan, sitting near him with my own bowl and making myself comfortable leaning against Zephyr.

Sen settled herself down on my lap, choosing to nibble on a few bits of rice from the stew while also dipping her feet in a bowl full of water again.

"We're still getting an influx of new residents and we're having to consider the possibility of making the Sanctuary shield larger, but already it is being noticed by the locals. Despite our hard-to-reach location, now the humans know about us, they find us. Either the magic of the shield is working less well, or there is mythical blood in some of the humans around here."

"They're not being quite so put off?"

"And they're talking about something being here. As if some of them can sense it."

I frowned. It wasn't good news and only made it even more pressing that I find a way to reduce the fear the humans felt for us.

"We've not been bothered by the agents to such a high degree, however," Lorcan continued, taking my silence as encouragement for him to continue with his information. "Either because of our proximity to you or because of your work exposing the agency and its methods, we are facing less danger than we have since we first met you."

"That's definitely something to be grateful for. But I don't think we're done with them yet. I rescued this group from them. And I don't think Jacobs has given up. He'll be plotting somewhere."

"You need to find him?"

"Yes. I think stopping him directly is the next sensible move. We need to be exposing men like him and hoping the humans will afford us respect and rights too." As I spoke, it gave me confidence. We were so close to being okay and able to live freely. We just needed to keep working a little longer.

While the Sanctuary was growing and mythicals were flocking to it, we were also growing in power and political weight. I was sure it would all help our cause. The more of us there were in one place, the harder it was going to be for people to not only ignore us but stop us from standing up for ourselves and keeping ourselves safe.

Minsheng excused himself partway into our discussion, yawning and desperate for sleep.

Over the next couple of hours, Lorcan, Zephyr, and I talked more, speaking of possible strategies and ways we could defend the Sanctuary. It wasn't long before dawn when Lorcan slipped into a trance and sat in one place for a couple of minutes.

I waited for him to return to the present moment, worried. The centaurs only seemed to pass messages like this when they needed them to travel fast.

"Refugee at the border," Lorcan said, getting up as he came back out of the trance. I hurried to my feet too, Zephyr and Sen right behind me.

"We'll come too. Just in case there's trouble," I said.

The centaur bowed at us as Sen bounded up onto my shoulder. As one we all sprinted for the door and the edge of the Sanctuary Lorcan had received the message from.

Although we had to weave in and out of houses until we were nearer the edge, we were coming up to the newcomer and the guard who'd found him within only a few minutes. The mythical looked to be part gnome and part something else I couldn't place. He was panting hard and clutching his side, blood visible on his clothes.

I rushed to his side while Lorcan walked to the border with Zephyr.

"It's all right; you're safe now. We'll get you patched up as soon as we can. How badly are you hurt?" I asked.

"I'll live, but it hurts like... Well, it really hurts."

"Lie back," I said, using my powers to lift him and carry him onto a makeshift stretcher and then lift that as well.

His eyes went wide at the effortless way I managed to move him, his body essentially floating along.

"Did anyone follow you here?" I asked as I walked beside him.

"I don't think so, but we were ambushed while trying to come to the Sanctuary. They got my friends and me and took us somewhere not far from here. There were other mythicals, and my friend, Harry, he... He tried to distract them. I was the only one who got away."

"All right. Don't worry. We'll rescue them," I said, anger beginning to fill me and make me wish I could do even more.

As I spoke, the air master appeared and took over my task, floating the young man away and giving me the ability to go to Lorcan. I quickly filled him in on what I'd been told, and the pair of us agreed that the guards should be extra careful, but it was unlikely that anyone was going to be coming after our newest mythical if they hadn't already shown up.

"Are you truly intending to rescue the rest?" the dwarf asked.

"Of course," I replied.

"But we don't know what kind of base it is and their forces," he pointed out.

"No, but we will, and I've never let fear of the unknown stop me from saving mythicals. There's not been a single thing the soldiers and agents have thrown at me that I couldn't beat."

"We should speak to the council first. I know you wish to rescue them right now, but we need to be careful,"

Lorcan said. "You may have survived everything so far, but we cannot lose you now."

I frowned. Lorcan had a point, but I didn't want to sit around and wait for someone to give me the go-ahead to try to find mythicals who needed my help.

"I'll scout. Gather more information and come back if we can't handle it," I replied before launching into the air. Zephyr followed, catching me as my head started to ache a little again.

You're not rested enough for this, Zephyr pointed out. *We're not rested enough for this.*

We can't let Jacobs imprison or torture more of our kind, I replied.

If we fight them now, we will just be handing ourselves to Jacobs as well.

Zephyr continued to fly in the direction the man had run from despite the reminder that we shouldn't act now. We kept low, but it was clear that we had no idea where we were going and what we were looking for.

After twenty minutes of flying here, there, and everywhere, Zephyr turned to head back to the Sanctuary.

We can talk to the council, gather some allies and get the refugee to guide us back out here, he suggested, no doubt to ease the sting of not finding the poor guy's friends. I could only yawn in response, my body reminding me that I'd already had a very full day and wasn't anywhere near as rested as I ought to be.

I gave in, annoyed at myself but knowing Zephyr was right. We couldn't find signs of a base out here without some guidance, and the sun was going to be in the sky soon.

We were out of time and didn't have enough information to work fast.

Lorcan still waited by the border, his eyes on the skies. I spotted the centaur a fraction before he saw us. Immediately he backed up a bit and gave Zephyr some space to land.

Touching down just in front of him, I slipped off Zephyr's back.

"Did you see anything of use?" the guard and council member asked.

I shook my head and yawned again.

"We should report to the council, and then you should rest," he suggested. I considered making the council wait for me to be there until after I'd had a bit of sleep, but I knew it would be considered rude, even if they deserved it for keeping me waiting in the past.

Lorcan came with me, neither of us talking as I tried to process everything that had happened in the last few weeks. It still felt as if I was always just responding to the problems as they arose and not getting ahead. Tracking these mythicals to a base and being proactive about taking them back would give me something to do.

The council was once more in their usual chamber in the cave, the whole area lit in the most amazing way, a combination of light reflected around as well as candles, a strange glowing insect and all sorts of other natural methods.

It wasn't as bright as outside, but it was light enough our eyes weren't strained, and everyone was in a much more flattering light.

Sierrathen smiled when she saw us and placed her hand

on the arm of the elf beside her to get his attention. He looked up and noticed me, and Zephyr and Sen as well.

Although the caves were mostly wide enough for Zephyr, I noticed the roof of this room was lower. He had to bring his head down a little to stop his horns from catching the ceiling. He sighed, but he didn't complain.

Lorcan moved from our side to take his seat on the council, and then they all gave me their attention.

"While I was near the border earlier this morning," I said, "your Sanctuary had an unexpected visitor. An injured mythical."

The council listened despite Lorcan having been present as well and knowing everything I said. I told them all I knew and the quick flight I'd performed to see if I could work out where the man had come from.

"What do you propose we do about this?" Hargread, the dwarf, asked. The shorter mythical had never been a fan of mine or particularly polite or kind, but I ignored the antagonism in his words.

"I will mount a rescue, either guided by or with the mythical in your infirmary," I replied. "Anyone who wishes to join me is welcome, as always, but I will make no demands nor place pressure on anyone. It will be a risk, especially after the recent developments."

"Your willingness to risk your life to help our races is greatly appreciated," Sierrathen said. "And I'm sure there are some among us who would be only too glad to join you. We will ensure everyone knows of your intentions."

"We will?" Hargread asked.

"Yes," Sierrathen replied without looking at him. "We do not control anyone here, merely offer everyone Sanctuary and respect. They all deserve to know when there are opportunities for them to act outside the city."

For a moment, no one said anything. I merely watched and waited, not wanting to interrupt what was clearly an important conversation. The silence soon grew awkward, however, and their gazes returned to me.

"I would also like to contact my friends at the warehouse. I believe some of them would be eager to aid me, but that can wait. If the council feels they are informed, I would like to perform a reconnaissance mission as soon as I can and then mount a rescue if possible."

"That sounds wise. We would appreciate any information you gain on your reconnaissance to be reported to us as soon as you can. It sounds as if there is an agency threat closer to the Sanctuary than we would like, and this has me very concerned," Vestan said, the only other elf on the council.

I nodded toward him as the centaurs often did and then backed up to leave while Lorcan continued to inform his leaders of the rest of the developments that evening.

Feeling very mixed, Zephyr, Sen, and I finally went and got some sleep. There was no way we could do anything to help anyone while we were so exhausted, even if I really wanted to.

CHAPTER TWENTY

"I'll be back as soon as I can," I said to Minsheng as Zephyr, Sen, and I prepared to fly off into the darkening sky along with our guest. We'd waited until the sun had sunk below the horizon and the first stars were coming out to be seen.

"Ditto. I'm sure some of the others will want to help rescue these mythicals if it's possible," my Shishou replied. He gave me a hug before walking out of the Sanctuary. He was heading back to the warehouse as swiftly as he could to get everyone prepared for a raid.

Once I'd scouted and the injured mythical with me had shown us the area he escaped from, I would return, and Lorcan would let Ronan know what we were planning.

Then we would mount our attack before anything else could happen to the mythicals who had been left behind.

"Ready, Rich?" I asked the injured mythical.

He nodded and made me wonder if he was putting a brave face on or he was one of the races which healed faster than normal. Although he'd had quite a serious wound on his side the night before, he appeared to be moving almost normally now. A bandage around his middle and a smaller one around his arm were the only signs that he wasn't fighting fit.

The man had a gnome-like face and was short but was otherwise fairly human in appearance. It made me wonder how the agency had realized he wasn't human, but now wasn't the time to ask him all the details of his capture. His friends were in danger, so we were going to try and rescue them.

Before long, we were up in the sky, and the man was clinging to Zephyr for dear life. I flew beside them, not wanting to tire Zephyr out by having two people ride on him at once.

"This is amazing," the guy said as he flew through the sky. I grinned, Sen tucked into my jacket again and my own abilities powering us through the air.

Although I couldn't fly for as long as Zephyr by a long way, this was still a great way for me to get around and scout.

With our companion giving us directions, it only took about half an hour to find the small base he was fairly sure he'd run from the night before. He seemed to grow frightened as we got closer, tucking himself in closer against Zephyr's back.

I took the lead, looking for signs of agents and soldiers on guard duty and anything else that might give us an indication of what we were up against.

This base was quite different from the last one. It was much smaller in terms of footprint, but it had two larger buildings with a few smaller ones dotted around. There was no way to tell how many agents and soldiers were inside them, but I could see at least one pair on the outside doors of each building.

Another couple of sets of guards stood in watchtowers on both the north and south edges as well. They would be the most problematic to get past. There were also a few cameras, but they looked older and easy to break.

Zephyr flew circles, coming down as low as we dared to try and get the best view of what we were facing, his eyesight by far the best of all of us. It wasn't ideal, given that we were trying to be careful, and the last thing we wanted to do was tip them off that I was around.

Once we'd gotten the complete picture, I had Zephyr land a ways back, and we tried to work out what to do next.

This looks a little too easy, Zephyr said into my head. *There were far more guards and agents and soldiers moving about the last time we took on a base. If they truly suspect they're near the Sanctuary, then they aren't looking to attack it.*

Yeah, I think you're right, but it probably means that they're up to something else. We're unlikely to find out what that is without going in.

I heard Zephyr let out a strange little growl. He clearly wasn't happy, but I wasn't sure what I could do about it. We needed to rescue the mythicals. And it wasn't as if we had lots of experience in this situation.

I know we don't have much experience, but if we go inside, we need to make sure we don't kill anyone, Zephyr said a little while later.

There was no disagreement from me. I didn't want to hurt anyone else or give the government any more reasons to hate us, but there was a good chance they had more of our kind in the compound. I couldn't leave them trapped like Emily had been.

We should try and find out for sure, but I still don't like this.

Despite Zephyr's misgivings, we did a large loop around the base, getting as close as we dared and stopping for a bit to monitor the traffic on the road in and out of the area.

There were only a few agents and soldiers going in or out, which was another sign it was likely to be fairly quiet. I'd also seen the agency turn up, and they'd escorted someone inside.

We'd been too far away for us to be sure it was a mythical, but it allayed Zephyr's misgivings, and even Sen approved the idea of us coming back with reinforcements.

I had also seen enough to be confident that a tactic similar to the previous occasion would probably work again, although I was hoping we'd have a few more volunteers willing to help us. Last time we'd struggled to defeat all the forces.

I'd also been shot. Admittedly I'd been wearing Kevlar, but I'd been shot nonetheless. There had been a bruise on my torso for well over a week afterward.

Back to the Sanctuary, I said into Zephyr's head as we took to the skies again. It was time to make a plan and let the Sanctuary know what was nearby.

The base was tucked out of the way, surrounded by trees and to the south of the Sanctuary. When we'd been looking for good locations for them, I'd not had the chance to check so far out in a direction we didn't normally fly. I felt a little guilty for not noticing the place, but as we flew away, it disappeared into the trees, small enough they swallowed it among their canopy.

I soon focused on what I was going to say to the council. Until I knew who was going to volunteer to rescue the mythicals, I didn't want to make any other plans.

All the way back, I could tell Zephyr wasn't happy. Normally the three of us chattered, but Zephyr felt to me as if he was brooding about something. On top of that, I had been planning, and Sen continued to stare in wonder at the places we flew over.

Only our extra, still riding on Zephyr, seemed to perk up. He was looking around in amazement and wonder at flying so fast through the sky.

I couldn't really blame him. It reminded me of how amazing it had felt to fly the first time I'd managed it. Already I'd begun to take it for granted. I needed to remember not to.

Lorcan waited for us just inside the Sanctuary boundary, standing in the shadows but still just about visible as Zephyr circled to land.

Touching down, I relaxed my control of the air around me and made a mental note to try and eat and rest my powers a bit before I led the rescue mission. I needed to have my abilities at their best.

I talked to Lorcan for a little while, telling him everything I'd seen and what I thought we were up against.

"That doesn't sound as bad as we feared," the centaur replied when I was done. "I will inform the council that we are unlikely to be overwhelmed by the inhabitants."

"I'm going to gather forces and plan an attack. I'd appreciate your help with the latter once you're free to do so," I replied. "I want to move tonight if I can. We've not confirmed the others are there, but it looks as if at least some mythicals are, but I think it's worth infiltrating anyway."

"We must tread carefully," Lorcan replied. "I don't want to give the American public a reason to dislike us further."

"Me neither." I looked at the mythical we'd rescued as he got down from Zephyr's back. He sported enough bruises and bandages over cuts that I knew we had to help his friends. I couldn't let the agents get away with hurting people like him just because they were different. Whatever I feared, we had to go ahead.

"Why don't you get some more rest," I said as he wobbled slightly. "We'll handle everything from here."

"I want to come with you," he replied. "I know I'm not in a fighting state, but I can be a lookout if nothing else, and I know some of the layout. I can help more than I'll hinder, I promise."

I wanted to say no. Not only had he been through enough, but I didn't need someone to protect. I knew how I'd feel being left behind, however, and he had a point about his knowledge.

"All right. I'll send someone to fetch you before we leave."

He smiled and nodded before he hurried off, and I watched him go. It was strange still seeing all the different mythicals in the city. Some of them looked so much more human than others.

Can we get something to eat? Zephyr asked into my head as we walked toward the guest house we were stationed in.

I'm sure someone will oblige us, I replied as Sen wriggled out of my jacket. She jumped to the ground and went scurrying off.

Sen find food, she replied, making me grin. Her absence gave Zephyr and me a moment to enjoy the peace and quiet of the Sanctuary and the natural beauty around us.

At some point, we should visit the Sanctuary just because we can and enjoy being here for something other than escorting people in or training or attacking something from here, Zephyr said.

Like a holiday? I replied.

What's one of those?

I'm not sure anymore. When I remember, I'll let you know, and we'll go on one.

Does it come with pizza?

Everything worth doing comes with pizza.

This is how I know we're soul mates, Zephyr replied, grinning at me. I found myself returning the gesture, but one element of his words stuck in my head. Soul mates. Did he think of us as soul mates?

I pushed the thought away. Now wasn't the time. Just like we didn't have time to take a break, we barely had time to think about how we felt about each other. Or anyone else, for that matter. We had to keep going. There were mythicals to rescue.

We found Seth, Gwaelon, and Dyneira waiting for us in the guest house.

"Lorcan said you've got more mythicals to rescue," Seth said, a light in his eyes I only ever saw when he was setting fire to things.

I nodded, smiling at him even if I didn't entirely like him. He was still arrogant, and I was never going to forget he'd told me to let Zephyr go as a bonded creature so someone else could claim him before he'd even asked my name or knew anything about me, but he knew how to fight, and he was sensible enough to take an order in the heat of battle. He was an ally I would accept.

Dyneira had also come with us the last time we'd attacked an agency compound. She was more than welcome. But Gwaelon was new.

"I thought you liked tending farms and staying out of trouble," I said a moment later.

"I do, but I also want to see Tuviel's heir in action. And Ruehnar told me I needed to help you start using your water powers too. He's got a bet going against the fire master over which you'll start using next, and I'll never be forgiven if I let Ruehnar lose."

I blinked, not having expected that answer at all. It spoke of the faith they had in me and made me wonder what I'd done to deserve it truly. All of this so far had been me getting lucky and being supported by amazing people. I tried not to think about any of the other elements.

"Well, while I'm not sure I approve of you all wagering on me, you're very welcome in battle," I said, trying to focus.

"Who else is joining us?" Seth asked. "Erlan complemented what I could do last time."

"He did, and I'm hoping he'll return with Minsheng and Ronan in the next hour. Minsheng should be back at the warehouse by now, and I believe Lorcan passed them the info we now have."

I looked at my small team and worried that we didn't have enough people. We'd had Crawley, Chris, and Daisy the previous time. Gwaelon didn't entirely make up for losing all three of those fighters.

Admittedly, Crawley had also been more than happy to shoot people, and we were trying to do everything we could to avoid deaths now. We couldn't afford to have more blood on our hands when the public wanted to accuse us of doing so unnecessarily. No matter how much we ended up in kill-or-be-killed situations.

My fears were soon allayed, however. Minsheng arrived along with Ronan, Erlan, Newton, Crawley, Daisy, Emily, Chris, and even Justin. Behind them was the new Shishou and the father elf we'd rescued the night before.

"We'd like to help," the new Shishou said, his eyes meeting mine with grim determination.

I nodded, appreciating the vote of support. I could only look around the group before me, blown away by the determination on all their faces and the growing group of supporters I had. We were going to be able to present an even stronger force than the last time.

Although I had some concerns about Emily and Crawley, Emily's arm was already out of the cast and sling, her own elven healing powers having kicked in and helped it mend combined with a little help from the elven masters at the Sanctuary. There was a very determined light in her eyes. The last time we'd been rescuing a mythical from an agency facility, it had been her.

Taking a deep breath, I drew what I could remember of the compound on the paper in front of us, adding in anything I'd forgotten that Zephyr remembered.

Finally, I marked the door that our escaped mythical said he'd come out of.

Crawley was the first to step forward and examine it.

"This wasn't a location I had any knowledge of," she said, "but there are a few things that I recognize as normal layouts and uses across all the agency facilities, so I think our best bet is to focus on that building alone. It will house almost everyone there."

Her information was more than useful, and it soon had the rest of the group speaking up as we planned the subgroups we'd attack in and where we'd begin.

We didn't think we could pull off the same trick we had with the first base, so we were all going to have to fight our way inside the compound. I was pretty sure I could lift most of the group up and over the fence if need be, but Chris soon stepped forward with several sets of wire cutters and some other cool-looking tools.

I noticed that there was a crate of fabric behind him. More of the stuff he'd had us wearing the previous night.

One thing was for sure: we were much better kitted out than the last time we'd attempted this, and we had another decent plan.

Once again, I looked around me at the faces of everyone who had volunteered to help. They all had the same determined light in their eyes. We were going to rescue more mythicals, and we were going to do it together. The human race couldn't keep us locked away or stop us from existing and defending ourselves. And they couldn't ignore us anymore either.

CHAPTER TWENTY-ONE

I placed a hand on Zephyr's shoulder as we walked toward the border of the Sanctuary, as much to seek comfort as to feel connected and make sure he knew I was in this with him. Once more, we were going to ride into battle together.

Many of the Sanctuary mythicals were still up, news of what we were intending to do having traveled among them. Despite the late hour and the unknown time of departure, they were up to wish us a successful mission and tell us to return safely.

Seth had fetched our wounded refugee a short while beforehand, and he fell in with the group while we wound through the houses.

I'd split us into four teams, a strong elemental elf going along with each. They were backed up by a solid marksman each and whoever else I thought would get along best with that team.

Trying not to think about what would happen if one of them died, we made our way to the border of the Sanctuary. This was it. This was when we showed the world what we were made of.

"Ready?" I asked everyone, giving anyone who wanted one a final chance to back out.

Most of them simply nodded. Ronan, Lorcan, and Dyneira gave me a brief bow.

With nothing else to say, I led them across the border, and Zephyr, Sen, and I rose into the air, Rich riding on Zephyr's back again.

Without me needing to direct them, the group split and went their separate ways. Several of them were taking transport to get closer. While they did that, Zephyr and my team would act as scouts, going ahead and checking the compound was still as we expected to find it.

When everyone was in place, we would use our communication stone with Ronan to begin the attack.

It still felt strange to lead people into battle, and I felt the weight and responsibility of keeping them alive. Someone had to lead, however, and it was clear I was the most powerful, even with elves such as Gwaelon coming with us.

You're also the only one with a dragon, Zephyr said into my head. *People like to follow a leader who looks the part too.*

These jackets Chris gave us do make us look pretty cool.

They make me feel pretty cool too.

I knew what Zephyr meant. Although Chris had given them a lining since we'd last used them, they still felt colder than clothing ought to. They were going to help keep us safe, however.

It didn't take long for the compound to come into view, Zephyr knowing exactly where to go this time around.

Despite the late hour, there were still plenty of soldiers on guard duty and agents coming and going.

Our lives had really become a thing of the night, all of our actions hidden from the general public. Although the agents had started it, I had embraced it. Acting at night gave us a safety net and an advantage.

Once we were at the base, we flew circles around it, keeping too far out for them to be able to see us.

I don't like this part of the plan, Zephyr said a moment later, feelings of anxiety and nervousness coming across the connection with his words.

Having to fly around in circles, or the waiting part? I asked.

Both. Circles are boring, and knowing that you're about to attack and not actually doing it is torture.

Everyone should be in position soon. At least I hoped they would be. My stomach was equally lined with lead and moving around like it was going to try and escape.

Thankfully, as we circled around again, Zephyr spotted the first of the vehicles carrying our friends. This one was an off-road jeep, and Minsheng, Ronan, Ellen and Daisy were standing beside it.

We swept lower and I gave them a wave, making sure they knew we'd seen them. Minsheng gave me a thumbs-up before the five of them set off, Newton sitting on Erlan's shoulder.

With one team pretty much in place, we flew on and looked for the next.

It was harder to spot the second group, their vehicle stopped under a set of trees. I could just about make out Gwaelon as he stood under the shadow of a particularly large tree.

Once again, Zephyr flew lower, and we let the group know that they'd been seen.

That left just one more group, the final set of people having farther to go.

They were also some of the most capable, and they'd taken the road most of the way.

As we flew around toward the compound entrance and the road that led away from it, we looked out for them as well. Not seeing them, I landed.

Not long after Zephyr had done the same, a couple of cars came up the road. They weren't the usual agency cars, and I was worried that innocent civilians were going to get caught up in a battle.

Stay here, I said to Zephyr as I quietly followed, keeping under the trees but getting close enough to the compound I could see the vehicles as they approached the gates.

A soldier leaned out of the window to talk to the guard on the gate, putting my mind at ease. I had no idea why they'd have such strange vans coming in at this time of night, but I was pretty sure we were about to find out why.

I hurried back to Zephyr's side, never liking being away from him. While I'd been gone, the final group had arrived. Zephyr now stood beside Seth, Lorcan, Justin, and the new Shishou and his elf, Jinto and Ascan.

"Now remember, while I don't care what you do to the property or the weapons, we need to make sure that we don't kill anyone," I said.

"Yet they'd kill us without a thought," Seth replied.

"I know. And it's not fair. But we need to win over the American public, and they don't. One day they won't be able to kill us at all. Until then, we have to be better than them."

Seth pulled a face but nodded anyway. Even if we disagreed, I was confident that he was going to respect my decision.

As Zephyr and I flew up into the air again, I could only hope that the rest of the teams would follow my orders to preserve all lives.

With everyone else in place, we also positioned ourselves in the sky almost directly above the compound. I settled onto Zephyr's back and held on tight. I pulled my communication stone from my pocket and concentrated on reaching out to Ronan.

I didn't want to be connected for long. There was a chance that Zephyr wouldn't be able to fly very easily while I was connected. So before it could connect properly and drag us both into some darkened room in our minds, I simply told Ronan we were already.

That felt weird, Zephyr said into my head. *I had to actively fight to stay in the present and flying.*

We didn't crash-land, so I consider it a success, I replied. I began counting in my head.

The other groups were stationed a little way out, so we needed to give them a couple of minutes to get closer, and then we were going to be the distraction.

Ready? I asked Zephyr as I lifted up off his back.

More than ready, he replied, a gleam in his eyes. We'd been hunted by the agents so many times there was a part of both of us that enjoyed dealing the same level of fear and aggression back at them.

There were probably people who wouldn't approve of

that, but they were the type of people who had never been scared for their lives or on the run and homeless and not sure where to turn. They were the sorts of people who had no understanding of what it felt like to be us.

As I finished counting out the three minutes we were waiting for, I dived downwards, feeling rather than seeing Zephyr do the same. He prepared to exhale a large cloud of the paralyzing gas he could create.

Although we were putting ourselves in danger by taking on potentially more agents than we could handle, we decided to draw all of their attention to allow the other three groups to come closer in as much safety as possible.

Because this compound was smaller and the fence was much closer to the buildings, there were no dark shadows to hide in while people got over fences or under them. And that meant we needed to make sure no one was even looking.

I jetted air out at the two guard towers and down at any guards I could see stationed on the ground. It wasn't an easy move to make, and I could feel it draining almost all my energy, but it allowed us to get down on the ground as quickly as possible without getting shot.

It didn't keep the guards from trying. Everyone who noticed us opening fire. The night was full of the thunder of gun cracks and chaos.

As soon as Zephyr was on the ground, he exhaled, and the refugee and Sen slid off his back and crouched underneath him.

I took control of the gas, moving it quickly over any guards that were nearby. I split off two large chunks of gas cloud and moved them as quickly as I could to the guard towers.

Our attack was so sudden that none of the guards near us had the opportunity to put on gas masks before they were knocked out.

I bought us a reprieve from the guards shooting farther out and circled us in a ring of gas as Zephyr exhaled even more.

They still shot toward our general direction, and I heard several bullets ping off Zephyr's scales. We'd put my Kevlar vest on the wounded refugee, and for now I was vulnerable, the tight band of air around me my only protection.

Pausing, I focused on keeping myself safe and powered up into the air again to try and get a better view.

The guards by the gate and the soldiers by the vans that had arrived just before us were shooting toward the team that was trying to storm the gate. Without hesitation, I blasted them with air and reached to control any plants nearby.

I'd soon ripped the guns out of the hands of the guards on the gate. The soldiers near the van had better grips on their weapons and were clearly more trained. Also, at least two of them stayed inside the vehicles.

Not sure what else to do, I lifted the vans with my powers and moved them to a rocky patch of difficult terrain among the trees just outside the compound. If they were going to protect whatever was inside the vans, they could do it from somewhere they couldn't get to us easily.

With the group from the gate finally able to get inside and most of the guards and soldiers outside of the buildings now neutralized, I returned to Zephyr and blasted the gas upward into the air, the vapor no longer useful.

Striding beside Zephyr, I made my way to the door the refugee had told us he'd come out of. Before I could get there, however, I heard an explosion, and heat rushed toward us from behind.

Whirling around, I saw a ball of fire spreading out from one of the cars near the gate. Newton was sitting near the flaming wreck of what had once been an incredibly expensive vehicle, but that wasn't what had drawn my eyes.

Zephyr's paralyzing gas was flammable, and a wisp near the car had caught alight as the gas tank had exploded. Now the fire was spreading into the air and around the gas cloud.

Before I could react, it reached the thicker section I'd placed at the top of a guard tower. Fire rushed toward the building, engulfing it and the guards within.

Immediately, I flew toward it, blasting the area with air to try and move the vapor out of there as I tried to locate the paralyzed guards inside.

The fire caught on the frame of the building, and all I succeeded in doing was spreading it farther. I flew up to hover level with the main section, still trying to identify the men, but I couldn't see them.

Not sure what else to do, I looked for Gwaelon, but he'd already run around to my aid.

I flew to the side just as water spouted up and into the tower from a nearby fountain. I felt the atmosphere change around me, the water elf literally sucking the water out of the air to try and make it rain in the tower.

Although it didn't entirely put the fire out, it cooled the

area and allowed me to fly closer, the flames on this side sizzling and trying to burn off all the water that had been dumped on it.

I spotted two bodies, both alight, and pulled them out of the building as quickly as I could manage. While I was still bringing them down to the ground, Gwaelon drenched them both, putting the flames out and showing their clothes had only just ignited.

Daisy rushed forward as I lowered them, checking both were alive as I got down to the ground. A soldier rushed up, a medical kit bouncing by his side and his weaponless hands in the air.

"They're alive but a little burned," she said to him, and he glared back before treating them.

"Daisy, help them. And Seth, make sure no one hurts her. Explode some more stuff if they do," I said. "Everyone else back on target."

I felt cold to be moving on so swiftly as I walked away, but it had been an accident, and it had already cost us two members of our team as they tried to make sure the men lived.

You're doing the right thing, Zephyr said into my head, stopping my anxiety and worry before it could fully form. We moved back to the compound and Zephyr leaned down, ripping the door off the hinges before exhaling into the building.

I tried not to grin at how efficiently he handled the situation. Now wasn't the time to be distracted by how proud I was of him.

Before I could stop her, Sen ran off into the gas, proving it had no effect on her once and for all. I sighed and stuck my gas mask on before taking control of the vapor and moving it ahead of me.

I went inside as soon as space cleared and ushered Lorcan's team and the refugee with me, the man now also wearing a mask. His eyes were wide, fear shining clear in them.

"Hopefully, we won't have to deal with anything else so unexpected," I said, trying to reassure him that we were in control. I wasn't sure he bought it.

Still, we had to continue, and I needed his direction.

"Which way?" I asked, hoping the others were managing to get on with their tasks okay.

CHAPTER TWENTY-TWO

Although I tried to leave a gap between me and the cloud, Zephyr added more in after us, making me grateful everyone was wearing gas masks. I fought to control all the gas, moving us in essentially a shielded area.

Somewhere on the other side of the building, Crawley was leading a similar unit inside. Although they wouldn't have the cover of gas and couldn't control it, they would possibly need their gas masks anyway.

Unfortunately, the corridors weren't wide enough for Zephyr to get inside, but he had another task to perform. I felt him get up into the air and fly over to the second building, my body seeming to tug in that direction.

Ahead of me, somewhere, Sen also scurried along, visions of corridors and rooms coming to my mind as she scouted ahead and projected her view to me.

We ignored offices, supply cupboards, and bathrooms while we looked for the rooms holding the other mythicals.

The building seemed deserted, making me feel bolder

as we trooped forward at quite a pace, directed toward the people we were here to rescue by their escaped companion.

Given how little resistance we met over the next few minutes, I began to worry that they'd been moved and there were far fewer agents here than there ought to be, but I didn't voice my concerns. We'd sweep the entire compound if we had to.

As Sen moved around a corner, however, she paused and dodged back. A moment later, she sent me an image of something flying toward her in a canister, smoke pouring out of it.

Run to me, Sen, I instantly said, but before she did, she looked around the corner again, a view of barricades and a structured defense in the heart of the building.

Immediately I stopped.

This made no sense. There would have been almost no time for the guards and agents to create something so obviously there to aid their defense.

"It's a—" My declaration of a trap was cut off as the refugee beside me lunged my way, something gleaming in his hands.

I spun, blasting air reflexively but still feeling a sting at my waist as Lorcan appeared nearby and I fell over.

Somehow I ended up floating, all my abilities now so instinctive I cushioned myself, and blasted more air at the refugee. He flew backward, smacking into the wall with a loud thud and a cracking sound. Going limp, he slumped down and a knife fell out of his hands, the tip of the blade coated red.

Putting my hand to my side, I came back with my own

blood on my hands, pain flaring where I'd touched and continuing to burn.

Aella? Zephyr's voice came into my head as I heard a loud, pained-sounding roar from outside. *You're hurt.*

It was a statement, not a question, but I answered in the affirmative anyway.

Stabbed. We've been set up. It's a trap. The mythical from the Sanctuary has just turned on us.

I watched as Lorcan bent down and placed his fingers against the man's neck. A moment later he straightened and looked at me, shaking his head, while Jinto rushed to my side and checked my wound.

"That's pretty deep, but I don't think it's cut anything too serious. We'll need to get it stitched as soon as we're somewhere safe," Jinto said.

I nodded and leaned back to give him better access to treat me.

Despite the pain and the fuss being made of me, I could only think of the man slumped in the corridor beside me. I'd just killed him.

Although I'd suspected I'd killed people in the past, this was the first time I'd actually directly attacked a single person and snuffed a life out. And I'd done it instinctively, no hesitation.

Tears sprang to my eyes, making the mythicals with me even more concerned, but I used my abilities to get me on my feet and push the vapor clouds back out to give us more space. I wasn't crying because I was hurt, but it was clear my companions believed so as they tried to clean the wound and bandage it.

I was more distraught by the wasted life. The mythical

we'd taken in as a refugee might have been trying to kill me, but he was misguided. I was no threat and no harm to anyone who didn't mean me any.

Frustration followed my sadness. Why did everyone see me as the enemy? I was just a girl from California who wanted to go home and run a dojo.

No part of me truly wanted to be a chosen one or a savior. I wanted to play games, read books, teach people to defend themselves, and fly over the sea with Zephyr. I wanted to be doing anything but fighting agents intent on hurting or killing me.

We need to get you some armor, Zephyr said into my head, ignoring my objections and refocusing me.

I'm normally wearing Kevlar, but he stabbed me below where it would be, I replied as I tried to focus on the here and now. It was clear I wasn't going to get what I wanted, and we had to get out of the building, if nothing else.

Now that the refugee was dead, I wasn't going to let him keep the protection I might need, however. Lorcan helped me remove it from the mythical and I slipped it on again, needing help while I was freshly injured.

The others don't know it's a trap yet, Zephyr pointed out. Before I could even think about how we might get to them, however, Sen came scuttling back through the cloud of gas and bounded up and onto my shoulder.

People coming, she said.

I reached into the gas cloud with my mind and felt the movement she was warning me about. Agents or soldiers were coming our way and fast.

"Incoming," I said quietly, trying to decide what to do

about it. I didn't want anyone else to get hurt for what had amounted to a trap.

Justin readied his weapon, a dart gun in his hands. I wished we'd brought normal guns and I had not bothered to save the two guards from the watchtower, but I knew that was one of the things the agents wanted. They wanted us to hurt them and look bad.

"What now?" the new Shishou asked as he got up from my side, the bandage tied off. "Do you think there are mythicals here?"

I frowned, not sure. There was no way I could know without checking the whole building.

Sen find out, my myconid said as she leaped down again. *Aella distract.*

Taking another deep breath, I focused on the approaching agents. We needed to fight on, but we needed to be smart too. They would clearly know we were coming.

I reached for my own dart gun and trained it on the targets I couldn't see directly, my control of the air showing me where they were anyway. I had to get them knocked out somehow, and then we were going to need to tackle the main group near the center of the building.

It might be a trap, but I was going to send them a message. No one got away with tricking me.

More to make the agents jumpy and focus on me than anything else, I shot in their direction while they were still in the thick cloud Zephyr had exhaled. I must have hit one of them somewhere important because he slumped and bashed into another. They both went down in a tangle of limbs and Sen used that moment to run past and off again.

I saw the view she had now and then but tried not to focus on it too much as I moved the gas cloud deeper and revealed the two agents. One was still conscious, but Justin shot him in the neck as soon as he tried to move.

He slumped to the floor, and I reached down and took both of the agents' guns. There was no way I was giving them a chance to wake up and come after us again. I'd take or destroy all the weapons they had at any opportunity. If I couldn't stop the agency, I was going to cost it as much money as I could.

Making sure nothing could set them off and emptying out the ammo, I dumped them into my bag, and then I focused on everything ahead again.

Sen had got past the two agents, but she was showing me an image of even more agents ahead. They were moving around and trying to get to us, the sound of the gun blasts no doubt having traveled around to them.

Not sure what else to do to hide her, I used the vapor from Zephyr and pushed it along the corridor so Sen would be hidden from view. I hoped it would work, but I wasn't going to stop pushing forward myself.

Within seconds I was aware of even more agents in the fog ahead and knew they were coming for us. As soon as they were enveloped, they did something I hadn't been expecting and started to fire ahead into the rolling vapor cloud.

Bullets flew toward us, my little team ducking and trying to get out of the way as I tried to blast them away. The first few shots got through, however, and I was knocked off my feet again, the Kevlar I'd just donned on once more saving my life.

I lay on the floor and checked that everyone else was okay. The agents continued to fire, and I'd essentially destroyed our neat barrier by blasting air at them in my panic. My friends shot back, however, and I picked up any bullet casings and debris I could see and pelted it at the agents using my airstreams.

I heard grunts and cries of pain before two more collapsed, one stuck with a dart and the other wounded from something that had cut across her arm. The paralyzing vapor had done the rest.

This wasn't going well. We needed a better strategy if we weren't going to get shot to pieces.

Safe again for now, I slowly got to my feet, an ache in my torso where I'd been hit. I noticed Lorcan's flank was also bleeding, one of the shots having grazed down his side. It had to sting, but the centaur was ignoring it.

In the meantime Sen had made it to the stairs and she was bouncing up them as quietly as she could, pausing now and then to show me what she could see with our mental connection.

I carried on, stopping at the next corner and trying to both gather up the fog I'd lost control of and use my abilities to detect the agents ahead.

Not far around the corner was the area Sen had originally warned me of. A group of agents formed up behind barricades where they were able to defend themselves far more easily.

We'd not been prepared for resistance like this. They were clearly not as surprised as they should have been by our presence, and given the way our refugee had turned on me, I was pretty sure they'd known we would come to rescue mythicals that didn't truly need it. I was going to have to work out what to do about it, however. Leaving didn't feel like the right choice, but I didn't want to put us in danger for nothing, either.

While Sen and the others were checking for mythicals and anything else we might want to know about, my group needed to deal with the agents nearby.

I reached into the area with my mind, taking control of the air. I considered trying to suffocate them by blocking the air supply until they used up all the oxygen, but I wasn't trying to kill them, and I had a feeling that would be too difficult. It was a large open space in the middle of the building.

It wasn't going to be like the fires at the Sanctuary the first time I had visited. I wasn't trying to starve an angry blaze of oxygen that was burning through as fast as it could.

No, I was going to have to come up with something far better than that. And I was going to have to do it quickly.

I couldn't gas them because they were wearing masks, and I didn't want to just sit the gas on top of them because they might get a lot more trigger happy, as the other agents had.

No sooner had I thought this than I heard gunfire from somewhere else in the building. It looked like Crawley had run into agents too, and that meant my thinking time was up.

Tornado, Zephyr suggested a moment later. *Mix in my gas and something that will cut them.*

I blinked. It was the perfect idea. But what could I rely on to cause cuts but not actually kill them? While I tried to think of this, I reached even farther into their area, trying to see if any of them were moving. I felt something living nearby. I realized it was several cacti on a small table.

Grinning, I took control of them and gently, one by one, made them shed their spines. The small needles were going to be extremely useful.

I started separating out the air near me. There was no aircon unit between the agents and me, so I had to do it the hard way and move the colder and hotter air around and put more effort into getting it to spin.

Thankfully I'd practiced for this, and I was strong enough to get a twister swirling in the middle of the corridor.

It quickly sucked in Zephyr's vapor as it powered down toward the agents. As it moved away from me, I had to stick my head around the corner just enough to see. It wasn't moving as swiftly as I wanted, but it wasn't a bad start, and the agents were reacting with fear, this monstrosity getting closer to them.

I concentrated on getting it to spiral faster as I reached and searched for more cold air to separate out and funnel into it.

A headache snuck up on me so gradually from all the concentration that I didn't notice it until it pounded, but by then I'd done all the work, getting the twisting mass of air and vapor up and over the barrier the agents had constructed and into their area.

The more open area must have had an aircon unit because the tornado suddenly spun faster and grew easier to guide, my control able to relax as it slid past the table of cactus and sucked up the spines.

I heard yelps and cries almost instantly, followed by thumps and smacks from agents being knocked out.

Feeling a little braver, I got to my feet and walked out from behind the corner and toward the central area.

There were a couple of agents still cowering over to one side, but the second I saw them I guided the tornado closer and used the same attack on them to a similar effect.

With the agents in the area neutralized, I finally motioned for my group to continue on. This might have been a setup, but I was going to make the most of the situation I found myself in.

Once again, we collected all the weapons and ammo, and I made a mental note to find some way to dispose of them that wasn't going to hurt the environment too badly. Would that even be possible?

Pushing the thought away, I focused on the task before me. There were only seven agents in the barricaded area, but I knew it could easily have been enough to defend the area for a while, given the firepower they'd possessed.

Lorcan kept a lookout while I investigated. Three other corridors split off from here toward unknown areas.

The tornado faded, and I pushed the vapor that was left up to the ceiling. It was starting to break down, which meant I was going to need Zephyr inside the building, or I'd have to open a window if I wanted to be able to gas any more.

And there was also Crawley to find. Although I hadn't heard any more shooting since we'd begun our assault, I had no way to know if her group were safe or not.

CHAPTER TWENTY-THREE

How's it going where you are? I asked Zephyr, Sen letting me see what she could periodically again now I wasn't concentrating on attacking agents.

Getting there, he replied. *Found a scientist or two and another squad of agents, but they're all out cold and lying on the ground here. Might be getting a bit wet. It's begun to rain.*

As long as they're alive.

While I replied, I imagined the dragon ripping chunks of the building apart. He'd been given the instruction to destroy as much of it as he could. No doubt he was tearing it apart with his claws and teeth.

When I heard another couple of shots, I knew I needed to move my group on with their task and just do my best. I'd rested for a few minutes while I'd tried to gather intel, and now it was time to move on.

Although I'd intended to head down a different corridor, I made my way toward the shooting instead, leaving Lorcan to watch our rear while I led the others.

Before I could find out where the gunshot was coming

from, however, Sen came across people, her sight flashing up in my head as if I could see or remember it. Unable to focus on two things at once, I had to stop and concentrate on the information she was giving me.

She'd found an agency training area or a lab. I wasn't sure which. Most importantly, however, there were elves in it. Or what appeared to be elves. I watched as they tried to control different elements, each one having different levels of success.

I could only stare, the shock of what I was seeing paralyzing me. Were these people who wanted to be here? Or prisoners forced to let the agency study our magic?

I had no way of knowing, but when I heard more shots, I knew I had to stop worrying about them for now. Although I had a feeling I wasn't supposed to get this far, I also knew I had to be careful or I wasn't going to get us all out of here alive.

If nothing else, Crawley's team needed some backup.

Be careful, Sen, but keep an eye on them, I said as I tried to slip out of the vision and back to my current location. I came back to see Lorcan staring at me, a look of concern on his face.

"You just stopped," he said, his voice quiet so it wouldn't carry to any agents nearby.

I quickly explained what Sen had shown me, but I did it as I reached to control the air around me again. I needed to get an idea of where the agents were before we walked into them.

More shots sounded ahead and to our right, an open door farther up the corridor coming into view. It appeared to be the source of the noise, so I motioned for everyone else to hang back. I wasn't going to risk them being shot when we didn't know what we were walking toward.

As I got closer, I saw another room, this one fairly narrow with another door out the other side. Agents were in the room and facing the other way, shooting out at whoever lay beyond.

I pulled the dart gun I carried for situations like this and quickly aimed at and shot two. Lorcan appeared by my side a moment later and hit the other two, taking them by surprise as they turned to see what was happening.

It was quickly over, and then everything went quiet. Still I didn't move, crouched by the open door, Lorcan pulling back a little so he couldn't be shot so easily.

I sighed and lowered the gun as I saw the people they'd been fighting. Crawley led her small team toward us, also relaxing when she saw it was us who had dealt with her problem.

Slowly, I got to my feet and moved in closer, but she was already disarming the agents and checking the room. I relaxed and reached out to Zephyr with my mind.

How are the other teams doing? I asked him, knowing he'd probably have an idea of where they were and what they were doing.

They've not met much resistance. This building is mostly barracks. Beds, showers and a canteen. A few offices, but most of them are empty, and there's nothing strange.

No, I think it's all in here. But I'm not sure if we were supposed to find it or not.

Film it. Like they've been doing to us. If we weren't supposed to see it, we can make sure the world does.

I exhaled, grateful that Zephyr was keeping his head.

Sometimes the decisions all got too much. Being careful not to kill any agents while trying to keep my team alive was exhausting.

With everyone from the two teams safe and mostly unharmed, I told them what Sen had seen, and we made a plan. Justin was going to film for us, probably the least skilled in battle. We were also going to split back out into two groups to form a pincer movement.

"If they've got more like me," Emily said, her fists clenched, "I hope they're treating them better, or there's going to be hell to pay."

Feeling her fury and grateful she was on our side, I nodded.

"See you up there," Crawley said as she led her group back the way she'd come. There was a set of stairs not far from where they'd come in, and Crawley was pretty sure they were fairly unguarded. It appeared that no one was supposed to have come her way.

That meant I was the most likely to face resistance, although Sen hadn't spotted much. Or if she had, she'd chosen not to project that image to me. I reached out to her as I led my team toward the stairwell she'd climbed.

We're coming to you, Sen, I said.

She smiled and sent me a warm feeling back, but that was it, almost as if she was also trying to be really quiet. Zephyr landed on the roof.

Other building cleared, Zephyr added. *Daisy and Seth are keeping an eye on the few loose soldiers outside. They're not acting like a threat, but I think if the tables appear to turn, they'll attack.*

Noted. See if you can find a way into this building up there and cause some havoc.

Gladly, he replied, and I could almost see the delighted grin on his face.

We made it back to the stairs without incident and I slowly climbed them, keeping a barrier of air in front of me just in case and preparing for anything. Now that I was more tired, I also kept the dart gun out.

I could hear movement as I approached the top. The sound of boots on the solid floor, but they didn't seem to be coming my way. Pausing, I listened as my team caught up, then we moved down the corridor. I still couldn't see Sen or the elves she'd shown me, but I knew they must be ahead somewhere.

It was almost worse not engaging with the enemy, however, and knowing they were somewhere ahead. Where were they all? What were they doing? And why hadn't we been swarmed as we had with other agency places?

Still feeling like something about the whole thing was off but equally committed to seeing it through, I carried on to the next corner and paused.

This time as I looked around the corner, I could see a group of guards standing on either side of the hallway, a door between them. One of them happened to look my way before I could pull back.

He opened fire and drew the attention of the rest.

As they shot at me, I also fired in his direction. My dart hit his shoulder, and a moment later, he went down.

I heard a loud bang from somewhere above, and the building shook slightly.

That you? I asked Zephyr as I pulled back a bit.

Yeah. I found a way in. Well, I made a way in.

I grinned as I imagined Zephyr ripping something off that had got in his way. He was so powerful now that buildings really didn't stop him most of the time.

As I heard the sound of running feet coming from somewhere else nearby, now heading our way, I frowned. Maybe we were finally about to meet the cavalry.

Lorcan and Jinto found a good place to shoot from while Ascan prepared to use his magic. All the while, Justin continued to film what he could.

Not wanting them to get hurt, I took a deep breath, focused on the air around me, and tried to feel for the agents. There was one more close by, just around the corner, so I quickly peeked around the edge and shot at him. The dart flew off course, but I managed to guide it and get the agent in the thigh.

He slumped as more agents appeared to one side.

I pulled back as they all fired down the corridor and then kept coming, rushing toward us. I didn't know how many there were for sure, but the noise of their booted feet marching our way was loud enough that it had to be more than a few.

Lorcan tried to lean out and shoot as well, but the quick return of bullets soon had him pull back as I tried to blast the air sideways and push the agents away from him.

Despite my efforts, a bullet narrowly missed Lorcan's face.

I needed to do something, or we were going to be slaughtered.

Thinking fast, I hurled air down the corridor and looked around again.

I was faced with eight agents, and while I blasted them with as much air as I could, I also fired. The darts caught two of them, but the bullets kept coming, and another hit me in the side.T Kevlar vest stopped me from being anything but bruised.

It knocked me back, but I pushed up from the floor with my powers, recovering quicker than before. I was starting to get used to being shot, something I'd never have expected to think.

As I got back to my feet, still blasting air down the hallway, I noticed the men all had a strange shield, similar to the ones they'd had the first few times I'd encountered agents, but when I tried to pull on them and blast them with air, it seemed to travel through and around. No matter what I did, each of the men could keep hold of their shield and stand their ground.

I frowned. It seemed they were learning from our encounters and adapting. Maybe they weren't underestimating me so much after all.

Still not wanting the others to put themselves in danger when there was such a high chance they'd be hit by a bullet, I threw up the thickest wall I could and tried to yank on the agents' guns instead.

The bullets kept coming, however, only one agent holding his weapon loosely enough I could tear it away.

It skittered across the floor toward me, but I didn't dare try and retrieve it yet. Instead, I shot more darts, using my abilities to help fly them past shields and hit the men anywhere exposed enough.

The advantage of trying to hit them with darts was that I didn't need to worry about where I hit them. As long as it pierced the skin, they were going down. Three more men were disabled, leaving only a few agents left, but my abilities were beginning to wane, and I was starting to get a headache again.

Another bullet hit my Kevlar, more square-on than the last one, and it knocked me back with an *oof*. My abilities entirely shut off, and I dropped my dart gun.

While I was gasping, more than a little winded, Lorcan rushed out and shot with a precision I wouldn't have thought possible, his shots hitting two more of the agents.

Someone grabbed me and started pulling me back around the corner, bullets whizzing past both of us.

I tried to get another air wall up or blast it at the final gun, but I just couldn't get anything to work.

Two bullets hit Lorcan full in the chest and he staggered back, almost trampling me before he collapsed.

"Lorcan!" I yelled but he barely responded, just giving me a nod, and then he was gone, his eyes glazing over, his body still on the floor.

There was stunned silence, none of us knowing what to do with one of us dead. I felt both numb and like shrieking. He'd just saved my life, and in doing so, had sacrificed his own.

Feeling anger flood through me as my vision blurred from the tears threatening to fall, I got to my feet, grabbed the nearest dart gun from where he'd dropped it, and hurled myself around the corner, shooting again and again.

The final agent tried to fire, but before he could, Sen leaped from wherever she'd hidden and landed on his head. She grabbed onto the agent's hair as he tried to reach up and swat her off.

As he did so, he dropped his shield, and I hit him in the neck with my last dart.

He went down as I turned to go back to Lorcan, barely able to see through the tears. I rushed to the centaur's side, desperately hoping I was wrong and he wasn't dead.

Jinto and Ascan had knelt beside him, however, and they stopped me from getting too close.

"He's gone," Jinto said, the Shishou shutting Lorcan's eyes for him before getting up.

"We should keep going and come back for him if we can," Ascan said, but I shook my head and sat down, tears streaming out of my eyes.

Aella? Zephyr said as Sen came slowly walking up and rested her tiny little hand on Lorcan's flank. *Is that...Lorcan?*

Yes. I shuddered. *Yes. Lorcan is dead.*

I continued to cry, losing all sense of time while I simply stared at the motionless centaur.

He was dead, and it was all my fault.

CHAPTER TWENTY-FOUR

I became aware of someone shaking me. I looked up to see Crawley. A moment later, Dyneira appeared and knelt in front of Lorcan, tears pouring down her face. Slowly she bent down and pressed her forehead against his, her face screwed up in a silent wail.

I wanted to join her, but I felt myself calm just enough to know we were still in danger. Somehow we had to keep going.

"We'll stay here and watch over him," Gwaelon said, nodding to Dyneira and standing by her, his hand on her shoulder.

Trying not to think how much more Lorcan would have meant to the people living in the Sanctuary, I got to my feet and backed up. Crawley put a reloaded dart gun into my hand.

"Do you need a snack or whatever you do to recharge?" she asked.

I frowned, not sure how appropriate it was to eat in this

situation. However, I had to keep doing my thing, and I had to make sure no one else died.

Feeling more numb now than anything else, I pulled a couple of snack bars out of a pocket as Sen leaped onto my shoulder and snuggled into my neck.

Somewhere I could feel Zephyr, his heart also hurting, but waves of concern also washed my way. He already had memories of deaths his ancestors had faced in the past. He didn't need another reminder of grief.

The ones in my memories are faded. I can look through them as if they're both mine and not mine, Zephyr immediately explained, showing he was listening in to my thoughts and checking I was okay. *This is fresh grief, but also your first. The first is usually the worst.*

Thanks, I replied but instantly regretted the snark I'd thought it with. It wasn't Zephyr's fault.

Lorcan did what he was trained to do and died with honor. He died defending someone he cared about. For someone like Lorcan, there is no more honorable way to go.

That doesn't make it hurt less.

No, it doesn't, but it does help you not blame yourself. He made the choice to risk his life for you. And the agent chose to obey orders to shoot at us. Neither is your fault.

I exhaled, aware he'd predicted where my thoughts had been going.

There are elves who need you. Make Lorcan's death mean even more by finding them and rescuing them, Zephyr added.

The words were finally something I needed to hear, and I took another couple of deep breaths before eating most of the snacks I had. Already I felt a little stronger. Sitting for a bit, even if I'd sobbed while I did so, had rested my abilities. Now I was ready to keep working.

After looking at the people following me, I led the way again, making sure the air wall moving ahead of us was thick. I was on the lookout for other threats. I needed to have enough capacity left to deal with any more agents.

As we rounded the next corner, we reached the lab area Sen had been showing me in her vision. There were two more soldiers, one on either side of the door. Before they could properly lift their guns, I blasted them with air and knocked them off their feet. Crawley and Jinto shot them both, targeting one each.

I led the way closer, wary once more, looking in through what appeared to be a reinforced one-way glass panel. The elves inside the room had noticed the noise, but it didn't appear as if they could see us.

I saw them all look around and talk between themselves, clearly trying to work out if they should be concerned or not.

As I went to open the door, I thought back through what Sen had shown me the first time she was here. What did they think of our kind? Were they forced into training for the agents, or were they here of their own free will?

Hesitating, I tried to clear my mind. This wasn't going to help me. I couldn't start doubting myself now, not after losing Lorcan and everything Crawley had said. If these elves wanted something else for their lives, they could choose that themselves once they knew what the options were.

Taking a deep breath, I stood and pushed at the door. It wouldn't budge.

Crawley pointed at a scanner on the wall that looked like it scanned people's eyes. Looking around, I picked up one of the guards nearby that we'd knocked out and got Crawley to help me lift him. Emily pulled a slightly disgusted face before she forced his eye open in front of the scanner. The door clicked open.

After putting the guard back down, I went over to it. This time I didn't hesitate to push the door open.

Instantly the men and women inside flinched and moved away. I'd scared every single one. They all wore a matching jumpsuit-style outfit, tracksuit pants, and thin tops with sleeves down to the elbows. A stripe of color ran down the side seam of each one.

"Hi," I said. "I'm Aella. You want to get out of here and go someplace where elves are safe or do you work for these guys and want to stay?"

The effect of my words was immediate. All of them rushed toward me, talking at once as they asked questions and pulled wires and patches off their skin. All except two people dressed ever so slightly differently.

Those two had a different-color stripe, and they glared at me.

As I lifted my hands to get everyone to stop talking and Crawley and Emily joined me in the room, I fixed my attention on the silent two.

"Are you the ones in charge here?" I asked.

One didn't respond, merely glaring at me, but the other nodded.

"What have they told you about me?"

"That you want a war with humanity and you don't

respect life. That you're going to get everyone killed, including our kind."

"Right," I replied, aware these two had probably drunk the Kool-Aid and were going to be hard to dissuade. But I had to respond in some way. I couldn't ignore the accusation.

I looked at the others, some of them now hesitant.

"Firstly, I don't want a war. I want peace. Now I know I can't prove that right now, but...this gun I'm carrying." I held it up. "Dart gun. I'm not killing anyone if I can help it. But down that hallway is a dead centaur. He was on the council of a large mythical haven near here. The Sanctuary, it's called. I don't run it or live there, but he did, and for centuries, they've been taking in mythicals and giving them a safe home. You're all welcome there. He died trying to protect everyone there and keep them hidden and safe."

I paused and looked around again, the faces now even more hopeful. Tears threatened to fall again. It felt both wrong and right to use Lorcan's death in an argument, but I knew he'd want me to try and convince and save as many of them as possible.

"Secondly, I won't make any of you do anything. I would never force you to do anything, so how about this? We'll all leave here. The building is about to come down one way or another. You can then decide what you want to do. And if you ever change your mind and want to come find the Sanctuary later, that's great too."

I knew the latter was a stretch. Technically the Sanctuary had just let someone in who had come from here, and they'd tried to lead us all into a trap. I wasn't completely sure these people weren't somehow part of that trap. They might even be tasked with causing more havoc. But I had to choose to trust other elves each time, or Jacobs would definitely win.

That they'd also been kept in a guarded area with a pretty secure lock made me fairly sure I hadn't been supposed to find this group of elves. We should have been captured or killed on the floor below by the agents who'd formed the barricade or the agents who'd defended the halls up here in greater numbers than we normally faced.

My reasoning seemed to have the desired effect, and the twelve men and women filed past me and followed Crawley out of the room.

I followed the elves out and then started checking the nearby rooms to see if there were any more. Instead of more elves, I found a lab or monitoring room and what looked like a server room behind it.

"Chris," I called, hoping he was close enough he could hear me.

The gnome appeared at my side a moment later.

"Whatever they're doing here, can you destroy all the information?" I asked.

"Maybe, but it will take me a few minutes. Do you want me to also see what they've been studying? It might be useful."

"Only if you can do it quickly enough."

"Aye, I'll do my best. Send the water elf in too. He can probably help me destroy the hard drives on any computers and the servers once we're done."

I nodded and moved back out into the corridors. I now had a group of almost twenty, and I was aware there might be more agents in the building. But I didn't want to leave Chris and Gwaelon without some support either.

A moment later, I also noticed that Zephyr felt close, the tug in the pit of my stomach nowhere near as bad as it had been.

Where are you, Zephyr? I asked, grateful Sen was back on my shoulder. Most of the elves were staring at me as I waited for him to respond.

About twenty yards from you. About to break into the corridor you're in. I think.

"Come away from that wall," I said as soon as Zephyr finished speaking. I waved the confused elves away from his position and threw up an air wall to keep the debris that might go flying away from the mythicals.

A few seconds later, there was a tremor, and the wall bent outward before crumbling. There were a few gasps and even more fear, the elves running to get away when Zephyr put his head through.

"Be with you shortly," he said, grinning at the way everyone had reacted to him.

Don't scare the new recruits, I said, but internally, I was laughing.

"It's okay," I said aloud to get everyone's attention. "Elves can bond with mythical creatures. I've bonded with Zephyr. He's here to help."

"Yes, I am only here for the pizza," he replied.

This made a few of them laugh and helped ease the atmosphere again.

While everyone gave Zephyr a bit more space, he pulled the wall out even farther until he had a wide enough gap to stick his head and shoulders through.

You might want to go back the way you've come and get everyone out of the building. I'll pick up Chris and Ascan and get them out of here once we've made sure this building is unusable, Zephyr said into my head.

I nodded and chowed down on another snack bar. It got me a few looks, but I quickly explained that eating was the quickest way to recharge our elven abilities. This seemed to be new to everyone in the room, including the two who had been in charge.

"Right," I said a moment later as Zephyr continued to widen his hole and Chris worked furiously in the server room. "Which ones of you can use air?"

Four of the elves came forward, three women and one very young man.

"Great. I need you to help me carry out all the paralyzed and tranquilized agents so they don't die while everyone else gets ready to destroy this place. Can you do that?"

They looked between each other and seemed unsure of themselves, but one of them nodded, and that made the others more confident.

"Don't worry, I'll show you how it's done," I said as I moved through the group and led the way back down the corridor. As soon as we reached a large group of fallen agents, I had the other air elves come and join me.

"Reach out and feel for the air around the agents, but don't try to control it. Just follow it as I pick them up."

I waited a moment and then lifted the men off the floor, one by one, until I held all eight up. The elves' eyes grew wide, and more than a few mouths fell open. It made me want to laugh again, given what I was capable of in other ways.

When they were in the air, I had the elves take over, holding one up each, and the most confident then volunteered for another.

Feeling the burden on my abilities lessen, I lifted the two we'd left behind by the research rooms and hurried along to the next section. There I found Gwaelon, Dyneira and Lorcan. Several of the elves visibly paled at the sight of the dead centaur and I felt my emotions begin to build again. I had to push them aside, however.

While we'd been gone, Dyneira had arranged Lorcan's hair, tail, and limbs so he appeared more peaceful and cleaned off the blood. It only made me feel even more deeply for them.

They cared so much about each other, and there were so few of their kind. To lose just one of them was heartbreaking in so many ways.

I tried not to think too deeply about it, moved to tears too easily still. There were elves and other mythicals I still needed to help.

Gently, I lifted Lorcan's body, doing everything I could to keep him pristine and arranged as Dyneira had. The centaur gave me a nod and walked beside him, her hand remaining on his flank.

Gwaelon went to Ascan, Chris, and Zephyr to aid them further, and everyone else followed me.

Along the way, we found the other team, and I lifted more and more agents and soldiers we'd knocked out. There were a lot more than I'd realized, Crawley and her team having taken out more than a handful or two as well.

By the time I had all the paralyzed or unconscious agents outside and lying in an orderly pile in the parking lot, I was exhausted, but I never put Lorcan down, or let my concentration on him waver.

Ronan's reaction was the worst. He tilted his head back and roared his anguish to the skies before going to Dyneira. They leaned toward each other until their foreheads met and placed their hands on each other's shoulders.

I gave them a moment, not sure what to do as Crawley and Minsheng worked together to organize our teams again and liaise with the few agents and soldiers who had hung back after treating their own wounded. As far as I could tell, the people we'd hurt in the fire were still alive, something to be thankful for. And Justin and Emily were still filming almost everything on their phones.

It didn't take me long to notice that Erlan was doing the same, and it made me sigh. How could any of this have come down to who could film the worst bits and portray the other so badly?

Daisy came rushing over to tend to the wound I'd received, quickly cleaning it and patching me up. Then she checked the others, giving Dyneira and Ronan space.

When Ronan and Dyneira parted, I bowed to them both, not sure what else to do, but Ronan came to me and repeated the gesture he'd just given Dyneira. I copied what she'd done, hoping it was respectful of me to do so.

"How did he die?" Ronan asked a moment later, his voice deeper than usual and cracking as he uttered the last word.

"He saved my life when a bullet knocked me off my feet and my powers failed," I replied, knowing I would never get a chance to repay such an act in the same way.

"Then he died how he would have wished to. In honor."

I nodded, and again the three of us bowed to each other.

"I will continue to bear him where you wish if that is appropriate of me to do so," I added.

There were no more words as Ronan inclined his head, then Zephyr appeared, jumping down from the building behind us. He had Gwaelon, Ascan, and Chris on his back, but all three slid to the ground.

"I disabled the water systems in the building as Chris suggested," Gwaelon said. "I believe the sprinklers are now no longer operational."

Erlan grinned as Seth also stepped closer.

"Burn it down," I said, only too glad to give the order. I then started the procession as all of us left, Emily still filming.

CHAPTER TWENTY-FIVE

All walking together, it took us at least an hour to get back to the Sanctuary, and I continued to lead the group, Lorcan floating by my side and Ronan and Dyneira both on the other side of him again.

Behind us came the elves we'd rescued and then everyone else, many of them keeping their weapons ready in case we encountered any other trouble along the way.

It was a sad reunion when we crossed the border and the news of Lorcan's passing quickly spread. Out of respect for the Sanctuary and under Ronan's guidance, I placed Lorcan's body down gently in the shade of a nearby tree. More centaurs gathered before anyone else arrived.

With my part done and the aches and pains I'd suffered growing worse as I grew more tired, I tried to focus on anything else. It was wonderful watching the other elves as they reacted to the Sanctuary and its beauty.

The two who'd been in charge still seemed as if they weren't sure about where they were and if they truly wanted to stay, but I hoped time would convince them that they were in a warm and inviting place.

It wasn't long before the council appeared, all of them together going to Lorcan as their priority.

I hung back, organizing with Minsheng for most of our humans to go back to the warehouse. There was nothing more they could do, and I didn't want to keep any of them awake any longer than necessary.

"Jinto said you were hurt," Minsheng said, and immediately Daisy appeared. I gave in to her fussing as she unwrapped my bandage and tended to the wound on my side. Already my powers had healed it a little, but she insisted on giving me something to numb the area before stitching it back up and rebandaging me.

"You want me to stick around?" Minsheng asked when Daisy had finished and everyone was heading back to the vehicles.

"No, it's okay. I'll fly back. And don't worry, I'll try to be careful not to rip a stitch."

"Oh, I see." Minsheng mock-pouted. "I'd weigh the dragon down too much."

"Well, I wasn't going to say anything," I replied.

"Too many dumplings." Minsheng grabbed his stomach before I heard Zephyr chuckle.

Zephyr then looked very serious as he lowered his head down to our level and looked Minsheng in the face.

"Are you saying I'm not strong enough to carry your piddly human body?" he asked, his voice sounding deadly serious.

For a moment, Minsheng didn't respond, possibly not expecting to have Zephyr give him banter in return. Inside

I was dying with laughter, but Minsheng soon tilted his head to the side.

"I wasn't going to mention all that pizza and what it was doing to your figure either."

Zephyr let out a chuckle before looking indignant once more.

"It's my wings. They make me look fat," he replied.

It wasn't only me who laughed at that one, and then the heavy atmosphere lifted a little.

Minsheng placed a hand on my shoulder and gave it a squeeze.

"I won't be too long," I said, with every intention of returning before the end of the night. I watched him go, leaning into Zephyr's side and wishing we could fly right after him.

A cough from behind me made me turn.

Sierrathen stood there, Vestan only a fraction behind her. Both elves had their hands clasped together in front of them.

"The council would like to convene with you and discuss tonight's events. We have many questions, not least of all what happened with Lorcan and why we have a dozen or so part-mythicals who aren't sure they even want to be here."

"It would be fitting for me to tell you of the heroic sacrifice your fellow council member made and the results of such an action," I replied, stopping short of telling them to shove their clear disapproval where the sun didn't shine.

So, the council chambers, then, Zephyr said into my head. *The sun doesn't technically shine there.*

Does the light that comes from the mirrors and lenses not count? I asked him.

Good point. They'll have to shove it somewhere more personal then. Might have to remove a few rods first.

I stifled my gasp. This kind of antagonism wasn't like Zephyr.

He sighed behind me as the council turned and led the way, Vestan lifting Lorcan's body in much the same way I had.

I'm tired of you being blamed, Zephyr added. *And of being treated like a mindless beast.*

You and me both, I replied.

Several other centaurs appeared while we traveled to the heart of the Sanctuary. Along the way, the elves were guided to a guest house, and others retired to either plan the funeral or to get some rest until they were needed.

I had little choice but to keep following the council, Sen on my shoulder and Zephyr at my side.

None of us spoke until we were all in the council chamber, Lorcan now laid out on a plinth in one of the main rooms. It appeared to be part of a burial rite or similar ritual they had for the dead, so I simply held back and let them mourn now.

As soon as I was in the chamber with the council, they demanded I explain everything. I'd been expecting it, but I still found it hard to talk about. And to make matters worse, not one of them gave me any encouragement or approval.

Their faces said everything.

"It's extremely clear that Lorcan lost his life while following you into a trap," Vestan said.

I frowned and opened my mouth to object, but Sierra-then held her hand up, essentially asking for quiet. The other council members looked at her and waited for some kind of indication she had something to add.

"Lorcan had a mind of his own. It would be disre-spectful of us to think he didn't give his life in a way he fully intended. We cannot rob him of his honor in our sorrow, and I caution against heated words that would do so."

I exhaled as Sierrathen finished speaking, grateful for her wisdom, but I still didn't get a chance to say anything else.

"With that said, it's clear that this was a trap, and this makes me concerned about your choice to bring the part elves you found here. They are not full elves and clearly have been working for the enemy in at least two cases."

"I would like to remind the council that I am also not a full elf. I'm not even half-elf," I replied, my voice firm as several of the council members were quick to agree with Sierrathen.

I finished speaking and looked at their faces. I wasn't sure I'd actually helped myself after all. I'd essentially just pointed out that I couldn't be trusted either.

"Aella is also part dragon and part human. On top of that, she had Lorcan's respect and trust, as well as Ronan's and Dyneira's," Zephyr said as he stepped forward. "She probably represents the wishes of more different races than any of us can."

His deep voice boomed around the cavern despite his talking quite quietly, and it brought all the focus to him.

Instantly I felt better. I wasn't alone. Zephyr had made sure of that.

"The council has most races represented well, thank you, dragon," Martyl said, the fairy more than a little unimpressed.

"Do you?" he retorted. "You might each be of a different race, but do you understand them all? Do you understand anything but what you think they should want and think they should be doing? How many new faces of each race have you met in the last week?"

"Your point is made, Zephyr, and it is a point worth considering." Sierrathen inclined her head in his direction. "I believe you are trying to tell us that Aella and yourself are out there bringing the mythicals in and caring for them, but you are bringing them here, are you not?"

"Yes, we are," I said. "Because you are doing a wonderful job in many respects. Neither Zephyr nor I wish to disrespect the Sanctuary or anything it stands for, but the times have changed. Humans know of us. And there will be risks involved in integrating with them. If you truly want what is best for every mythical in this world, you need to be open to listening to them even when they disagree with you."

I thought I saw Vestan smile. Sierrathen nodded, but the rest seemed less convinced.

"Either way, I didn't come here to argue," I continued. "I did what I thought was best at the time in a difficult situation. Whether it was right or wrong remains to be seen, but speculating does no good for anyone. If you feel the need to keep an eye on the new elves who have arrived here tonight, I will not try to persuade you otherwise. But know that how you treat them is how they will see the elven world. They already know the human one. It is your duty to show them something better if you truly believe what's here is better."

"Yes," Sierrathen replied. "You are correct. Lorcan was on our council because he was good at making the decisions needed in the heat of the moment and understanding how a decision in battle when people's lives were in danger is different from a decision that can be made as a group while it has all the time it needs to debate. His ability to do both will be sorely missed."

I exhaled, feeling some of the tension leave my shoulders. It was an acknowledgment of sorts.

"Perhaps it would be more helpful if we discussed what we are going to do long-term. The Sanctuary grows more full by the day. And there seems to be no decline in the attacks from these agents," Vestan said.

"We're going to need to work together to tackle this issue," I replied. "I believe it's two-fold. There's the government, who doesn't approve of us. Led by Jacobs, as far as I can tell. And the public perception of us, which has been swaying toward the negative. Fueled by badly cut videos of conflicts and accusations of crimes we're not answering for. I am working on both, but I cannot do it alone. I cannot even find Jacobs."

"That might be something we can help with," Martyl said a moment later.

I blinked at the fairy, more than a little surprised.

"Thank you," I said a moment later. "That would be of great use."

"Good." Sierrathen got to her feet. "Then for now, we

will attend to the last rites of our friend, and I know you must be tired. Once we have all mourned and we have given these new elves a chance to settle here if they wish, we will come together again to discuss how to tackle this problem once and for all. Perhaps, Aella, you could bring more of your advisers with you next time. I understand you have several dwarves, gnomes, and humans as allies."

"I do," I replied, stunned that their opinion was being sought. Perhaps I had been too hasty in thinking the council cared for no one but those in the Sanctuary. Or Zephyr's words had got through to them.

Either way, it was time to go for now, and I was more than eager to return to the warehouse to rest and heal. My side ached, and my head pounded.

It felt as if we'd scored a victory today, especially given the compound we had shut down and what had been happening there. I didn't doubt that it wasn't the only one. Somewhere, they would be experimenting on other elves, and the thought chilled me. It was time to expose this whole thing as swiftly as we could.

But for now, to the warehouse and bed. Walking out of the cave and back out into the open felt like it took an age and once again reminded me that Lorcan was gone and there were more than a few mythicals mourning his death. I nodded at Ronan once more.

"I'll stay here for now, if that's acceptable," he said.

"Of course. Your grief is valid and right, Ronan. You're always welcome, but you're never trapped. Know you belong in both places with nothing but trust and respect."

"Thank you, Aella. I am glad that Lorcan's legacy is

saving you. I know his worth has increased and will increase with all you continue to do."

I nodded, unable to reply to such a statement of faith. It was a weight of its own, as well, and I wasn't sure I was ready to think like that. I might have told the council that I had faith in my decisions, but it wasn't the entire picture. There was always doubt. Always a little voice that questioned. And more than a few stabs in the dark to try and find the right path.

With the desire to leave the Sanctuary now even stronger, we walked out into the night air and I inhaled deeply. It had been a very eventful night.

Zephyr didn't need more than a look from me to know I was ready to fly, and he ushered me onto his back before launching into the sky, his wings as they moved through the air a comforting and familiar sound.

Within seconds I was settled in my usual spot, Sen tucked into the top of my jacket and the three of us heading back to the warehouse.

Pizza? Zephyr asked a moment later.

I grinned. Pizza sounded great.

EPILOGUE

As a bang on my bedroom door woke me up for the third time, I groaned and rolled over.

Not again, Zephyr said into my head, also stretching and standing. Sen seemed to sigh where she'd been standing on the shelf, her feet in the dirt of her own little plant pot.

All three of us moved to the door as I opened it up. Daisy stood there.

"Sorry, Aella, but they've leaked even more. And...they've, I dunno, cut it or something. They've made it look like you deliberately set that guard tower on fire."

Shitsticks.

I nodded and frowned before following her back downstairs. Minsheng, Chris, Crawley, and Emily were in the kitchen already, everyone looking tired and worse for wear. Not long after I entered, Erlan followed, yawning and bringing his laptop. Daisy was just behind him.

On the TV was the clip that Daisy had just been telling us about. I watched as Minsheng rewound it and played it from the beginning for my benefit.

"Leak what we have," I said as soon as it was done.

"All of it?" Erlan asked.

"All of it. Every single bit. And issue a statement with it that when we left the scene, neither of those men were dead, and we fought to stabilize them both too. Tell them everything and then focus on the elves they had locked up, the photos of my wounds and bruises, and Lorcan's death in my defense."

Immediately Emily sat down next to the young elf, and the two of them started working together. They'd collectively become our social media experts and the ones handling our PR. It was sad that it was necessary, but I was going to fight Jacobs however he attacked me.

"You should offer them an interview," Chris said. "Offer to publicly tell people what happened, like you did with the investigation. And get a medical professional they can trust to check you over."

I frowned, not sure any of that was a good idea, but knowing I couldn't do anything without speaking to our little lawyer again.

"Phone Robert," I added. "Let's see what he thinks we should say. And if we're all going to keep getting dragged out of bed, let's at least have breakfast."

This was met with a chorus of cheers and everyone made themselves busy, either helping cook or doing other stuff.

"I'm going to keep looking through the data and info from their little research project. See if there's anything in there I can find to make them look even worse," Chris said a moment later. "Then I'm going to get back to working on some more tech for you. I've got a few more ideas based on stuff they had at that compound."

"All right, but mostly defensive stuff and nothing that can kill. Even accidentally."

Chris nodded, but the frown that went with it said it all. We were having to be so much more careful than them, and it wasn't fair.

I sat down and opted to help Emily and Erlan while we waited for the lawyer, but I was the first to my feet when there was a loud knock on the front door.

Minsheng came with me, as did Zephyr and Sen, when I went to answer, hoping my lawyer was proving to be as efficient and punctual as he had been the last time.

Instead, I was met with the flashing lights of cop cars and a group of six cops with about twenty armed soldiers behind them, all of them with their guns out. Behind them were at least three film crews.

"Don't answer the door," Minsheng said, going to do so instead.

I stopped him, understanding hitting me.

Do you trust me? I asked Zephyr while Minsheng looked at me, waiting for an explanation.

Of course. And I agree anyway.

"Aella?" Minsheng asked. "Are you seriously—"

"Yes. It's clear why they're here, and maybe this will work in our favor. They'll feel like I'm answering to someone."

"But it won't be fair."

"It will have to be, or I'll expose that too."

Without another word, I strode forward and opened the

door. There were flashes of lights as people took photos, as well as shouts from the camera crews. The cops made them quiet down so they could be heard. I didn't speak and Zephyr stood beside me, his body close and warm. Sen perched on my shoulder and held onto my hair as usual.

"Aella-Faye Carter, you're under arrest under the terrorism act. Do you understand?" the nearest cop said, his face serious and a sneer on his face.

I looked past him at one of the cameras, making sure my voice was loud and clear.

"I understand that I'm being asked to answer for perceived crimes. While I could resist all of you if I wished to do so and am powerful enough to make it stick, Zephyr, Sen, and I will come with you and cooperate with your investigation. We'd appreciate the opportunity to answer the accusations being leveled at us and to know the truth and justice prevail in this situation."

"The dragon and...whatever the creature is on your shoulder have to stay here," the cop said, reaching for his gun.

"They can't. We're bonded. If I come with you, so do they, or you will kill all three of us," I replied.

There was a hesitation again, despite this being a reiteration of something I'd said in front of many cameras before.

"Do you want me to come with you or not?" I asked a moment later.

The cop finally nodded and reached for his cuffs.

"There's no point using those," I added. "I can break them with nothing but my powers."

The cop looked to the one beside him and shrugged.

"If she's coming quietly, she's coming quietly. We don't always use them," the cop to his side said barely above a whisper.

"All right. This way, ma'am. Can the dragon fly after us? Or walk, or something?"

I looked at Zephyr, who nodded his head down.

"I can fly," he said.

More cameras flashed and one of the cops placed his hand on my arm, although it betrayed a tremble. I let him guide me through the crowd as the cops and soldiers parted for us.

"You have no reason to fear me," I whispered so only he would hear. "I truly have no desire to harm anyone."

He looked at me, his eyes searching me for something.

"That might be so, but I've been ordered to arrest you, so I'm doing it."

"I understand," I replied, knowing how much I'd looked up to the police at one time in my life. "And I know you do a tough job. You have my respect, Officer."

Within seconds he had me beside the cop car and was helping me into the back, careful not to dislodge Sen from my shoulder. I moved us inside without resistance, looking around and wondering what criminals had been held there in the past.

As the cops got inside as well, Zephyr launched into the air, and I felt him rise up to fly just above us. Within seconds we were on the move, and I was officially under arrest.

DRYAD SOULED

The story continues with *Dryad Souled*, book 6 in the Dragon of Shadow and Air series, coming soon to Amazon and Kindle Unlimited.

ACKNOWLEDGMENTS

Another massive thank you to everyone at LMBPN for making another book in the series happen. I love these characters so much and you help get them out there to readers who love them just as much. I really can't express my gratitude enough.

To Ella for yet more editing genius. You always make the stories and characters I write so much better than they could be otherwise. And you keep me on my toes and learning even after a decade of practice.

To Anne for my book dragon who keeps me company while I write these stories.

To Bear, for always being supportive and not minding when I plot spoil and tell you things in latter books to get my head around them and simply make sure I'm not the only person who knows.

To Phil for putting up with the chaos that's in my head and for not minding when I'm not always 'there'.

To the tiny humans, for reminding me that sometimes

it takes a hundred attempts for someone to learn something and sometimes it just clicks and you get it first time. And to God, for knowing what's in my heart.

ABOUT THE AUTHOR

Jess was born in the quaint village of Woodbridge in the UK, has spent some of her childhood in the States and now resides near the beautiful Roman city of Bath. She lives with her husband, Phil, her two tiny humans (one boy and one girl) and her very dapsy cat, Pleaides.

During her still relatively short life Jess has displayed an innate curiosity for learning new things and has therefore studied many subjects, from maths and the sciences, to history and drama. Jess now works full time as a writer and mummy, incorporating many of the subjects she has an interest in within her plots and characters.

When she's not busy with work and keeping her tiny humans alive she can often be found with friends, playing with miniature characters, dice and pieces of paper covered in funny stats and notes about fictional adventures her figures have been on.

You can find out more about the author and her upcoming projects by joining her on facebook, by watching her live D&D streams, or emailing her via books@jessmountifield.co.uk. Jess loves hearing from a happy fan so please do get in touch!

Jess is also opening up her discord for fans to come chat about what she's up to, and see a few sneak peaks of future work. There's also a chance to become one of her beta readers. If you'd like to check that out you can do so here.

CONNECT WITH JESS

Connect with Jess Mountifield

Mailing list sign up
Facebook group.
Discord group
Actual play D&D stream: Twitch or Youtube
Email address: contact me here.

BOOKS BY JESS MOUNTIFIELD

Already published

Urban Fantasy

Dragon of Shadow and Air:

Air Bound

Shadow Sworn

Dragon Souled

Earth Bound

Night Sworn

Fantasy

Tales of Ethanar:

Wandering to Belong (Tale 1)

Innocent Hearts (Tale 2 & 3)

For Such a Time as This (Tale 4)

A Fire's Sacrifice (Tale 5)

Winter Series:

The Hope of Winter (Tale 6.05)

The Fire of Winter (Tale 6.1)

Guild of the Eternal Flame:

Wayfarer's Sanctuary

Protector's Secret

Healer's Oath

Other Fantasy:

The Initiate (under Holly Lujah)

Writing with Dawn Chapman:

Jessica's Challenge (#5 in the Puatera Online series)

Dahlia's Shadow (#6 in the Puatera Online series)

Lila's Revenge (#7 in the Puatera Online series)

Sci-Fi:

Fringe Colonies:

Alliance

Haven

Rebellion

Rebirth

Reclamation

Star Trail:

Hunted

Sherdan series:

Sherdan's Prophecy

Sherdan's Legacy

Sherdan's Country

Sherdan's Road (A short story in the anthology 'The End of the Road')

The Slave Who'd Never Been Kissed (A short in the charity anthology 'Imaginings')

New Beginnings

Santa's Little Space Pirate

In the multi-author Adamanta series:

Episode 1 – Adamanta

Episode 3 – Excelsior

Episode 8 – Phoenix

Episode 13 – New Contacts

Episode 17 – Sacrifice

Other:

Clues, Claws and Christmas

Non-Fic:

How to Write Lots, and Get Sh*t Done: the Art of Not Being a Flake

Find purchase links here

Coming soon:

Urban Fantasy:

Dragon of Shadow and Air:

Water Bound

Day Sworn

Fantasy

(Tales of Ethanar):

The Pursuit of Winter (#2 in the Winter series, Tale 6.2)

Books under Amelia Price

Mycroft Holmes Adventures:

The Hundred Year Wait

The Unexpected Coincidence

The Invisible Amateur

The Female Charm

The Reluctant Knight

The Ambitious Orphan

The Unconventional Honeymoon Gift

The Family Reunion

The Immortal Problem

Coming soon:

The Unremarkable Assistant

OTHER BOOKS FROM LMBPN PUBLISHING

Sign up for the LMBPN email list to be notified of new releases and special deals!

https://lmbpn.com/email/

For a complete list of books by LMBPN please visit:

https://lmbpn.com/books-by-lmbpn-publishing/